BIG MAN

Matthew J. Metzger

A NineStar Press Publication

Published by NineStar Press
P.O. Box 91792,
Albuquerque, New Mexico, 87199 USA.
www.ninestarpress.com

Big Man

Printed in the USA
SunFire Press Imprint
First Edition
April, 2018

Print ISBN: 978-1-948608-42-8

Also available in eBook, ISBN: 978-1-948608-38-1

Warning: This book contains off-page teenage sexual behaviour, scenes of humiliation related to teenage bullying, depictions of homophobia/transphobia, and internalized hatred.

Prologue

THIS WAS HOW everything started—on a Friday afternoon, at the very end of school, three days into the summer term and in the middle of an unreasonable, unseasonable heatwave. It had been a Friday like any other until Tom Fallowfield stuck his boot in.

Literally.

It went a bit like this, to Max's admittedly patchy memory of the entire incident.

At three thirty-one, the bell rang, and he was dismissed out of his maths class. Friday was a notorious day for people being bored and at a loose end, so Max had (as was his habit) hurried off to his locker to try to get out of school before anyone caught up to him.

At three thirty-six, Max reached his locker. His fingers fumbled with the lock in a hurry, the metal loose in his grip because it was so ridiculously hot. Sweat was dampening the hair at his temples.

At three thirty-eight, his fingers slipped on the waxy cover of his geography textbook and sent the whole pile tumbling to the floor.

And at three thirty-eight and a half, a dirty Adidas trainer pressed down on said textbook just as Max reached for it.

That was kind of when Max knew he was a bit fucked.

"All right, Fatso?"

He didn't have to look up. The trainer narrowed it down to one of two people who would stomp on the textbook he was trying to pick up, and the deep, drawling voice—like some villain out of a film—narrowed it down to one. Jazz Coles. And Jazz Coles was bad news.

Max swallowed convulsively and gathered the rest of his things to his chest protectively. He staggered back to his feet and turned to shove them all back in his locker. His hands were shaking. There was sweat breaking out on the backs of his thighs and under his arms, pooling in the joints and fleshy bits.

"Oi. You gone deaf, Fatso? All that grease clogged your ears?"

"M'just in a hurry, Jazz," he mumbled.

"You what?"

"I said I'm just in a hurry," he said a bit louder and squashed his other books into the locker haphazardly. The corridor was slowly emptying, and the emptier it got, the faster his heart was beating.

"You're fucking rude, you are. You ought to look at someone when he's talking to you. You want Tom to teach you some manners? Tom's good with manners."

"Sorry," Max mumbled, turning hastily before the threat could be carried out. The metal of his locker bit uncomfortably into his back, pressing grooves into his skin, and he could feel his shirt beginning to stick to him. "I'm in a rush, that's all."

All three of them were there. Jazz Coles, Aidan Hooper, and Tom Fallowfield. Fallowfield was in Max's year, the other two the year above. They went to some football club or something together—Max wasn't sure. All he knew was that Jazz was the clever one, with the orders and the insults, while Aidan was the sidekick who screeched like a hyena and kept them supplied in fags and weed on a regular basis from his older brother's grow. And Tom...

Tom was the dangerous one. When the insults stopped, Tom started. And nobody wanted Tom to start anything.

"Not got time to talk to us, then?" Jazz drawled. "Why's that? You busy?"

"I—yes. Yes, just busy, that's all, busy weekend…"

"Busy doing what? Got a new girlfriend?"

Tom snorted. Aidan cackled and said, "Eurgh, Jazz, man, I'll bring up my lunch."

"Imagine that sweaty sack of lard slithering and grunting on some poor girl. You'd crush her, wouldn't you, Farrier?"

Max's face heated up, and his hair stuck to his scalp. He could faintly smell his own underarms, and the metal gluing shirt to back was beginning to heat up too, at Jazz's cool, slow delivery.

"Fatso Farrier, the flat-fucker. 'Cause that's what she'd be once you were done. Best stick to boys, yeah? Let your boyfriend fuck you, then nobody'll suffocate."

"I don't have a girlfriend. Or a boyfriend."

"Would you like one?"

"I—no, I, uh—"

"Just as well," Jazz continued blithely. "Nobody has a drowning-in-folds fetish. So if it's not a girlfriend or a boyfriend with some sick kinks, why're you too busy to talk to us?"

The corridor was empty. Max started to panic.

"Answer me, Farrier!"

"I—just—plans, you know, plans…"

"What plans? Sale on at Greggs?" Jazz asked. "New bakery opened up? Or is Mummy taking pity on her lonely little wobblebottom, and baked you a chocolate cake?"

Aidan gave a whooping cackle, and Jazz kicked the forgotten geography book towards Max. It skittered across the dusty floor, hitting Max's shoe with a dull thump.

"Best not leave that here," Jazz said. Hands in his pockets, pale face regarding him through narrowed blue eyes, he looked calculating—and Max couldn't figure out what he was calculating. "Oi! Fatso! Pick it up, then."

"Thank you," Max mumbled, hoping it would buy him a bit of a reprieve from...whatever Jazz was planning, and stooped to pick it up. His fingers scrabbled uselessly on the plastic cover, wet with anxiety.

"Thank you?" Jazz echoed. "Very polite, Fatso. Might want to make it sound fucking sincere next time."

"Here, Jazz, fancy a game?"

That deep rumble was the only warning Max got before Tom's boot—because of course Tom, totally mad, sadistic Tom Fallowfield, wore boots to school on a regular basis— connected with the side of his head.

Hard.

Max would have liked to say that pain exploded in his head, that he saw visions of God or heard the heavenly choir, that it was like dropping into a Tim Burton movie.

Actually, he just heard a massive bang.

And then he woke up in the back of an ambulance and knew he was in deep shit.

That was how it started.

Chapter One

"MAX, GET YOUR trainers on and let's go."

Max blinked at the suddenly open bedroom door and Aunt Donna's skinny frame doing an impressive job of filling the gap.

"Go where?"

"I have errands to run, and as your mum's at work and you're not, you're going to help me."

"But Mum said I'm supposed to rest."

"You're perfectly fine," Aunt Donna retorted. "They only kept you in to stop your mum fussing so much. There's nothing wrong with you. Now get a T-shirt and shorts on and get in the van."

"In the van? We're going out?"

"That would be why you need trainers," she returned and stalked out. Aunt Donna stalked most places, so Max tried not to take it personally, but...still. He had a headache. She'd have a headache too, if Tom Fallowfield had kicked her in the head with a pair of brand new Timberlands on.

But then, there was no arguing with Aunt Donna, so Max heaved his bulk off the bed—which groaned appreciatively—and switched off the TV. He'd been working his way through *Ashes to Ashes*, one of Aunt Donna's favourites, but it would have to wait.

Max had been taken to hospital, because Tom had knocked him out. Mum had cried her eyes out, and they'd kept him in until Saturday lunchtime before releasing him.

He'd just had a headache anyway, the doctor said, and he ought to be more careful when larking about with his friends. But it wasn't the headache that was worrying Max. It was the whole kicked in the head thing. On purpose. He'd never lark about with Tom Fallowfield—he wasn't suicidal.

Tom had never kicked him in the head. Shoved it into the urinals in the boys' toilets occasionally, and he'd pissed on him once doing that too, but he'd never kicked him in the head. And Max could remember Jazz laughing. Jazz had thought it was hilarious, and what if it wasn't just a one-off? What if...?

"Max! Hurry up!"

Max pushed away the what-ifs and pulled on a pair of shorts, the waistband cutting a groove into his gut. They were meant to be baggy, but weren't really, and bunched up his boxers uncomfortably. The T-shirt was properly baggy, but the slogan had stretched from Max's body forcing the shirt to expand with it, and the letters were misshapen and grotesque. Even his trainers were sagging. His fat ankles had pushed the tops open too wide, the laces struggling to hold the shoes tight over his boat-like feet.

But Max was used to all that. It was the heat when he lumbered downstairs and stepped out of the house that nearly knocked him flat.

"Oh my God," he said to Aunt Donna, who was already in the driver's seat of her battered work van. She smirked and jerked her head at the passenger seat, big sunglasses already in place.

"Bit warm, isn't it?"

The T-shirt was already sticking to Max's chest, sweat lines beginning to form under his breasts—and yes, he had them. Jazz particularly enjoyed throwing water at him at school so they'd show through his white shirt, and calling him a lardy girl disguised as a lardier boy. The seatbelt didn't help, plastering a thick damp line right between them. Max rolled his window all the way down, barely resisting the urge to stick his head out like a dog, as Aunt Donna rolled the van backwards off the driveway and forced it into gear with a hefty *clang*.

"How's your face feel?"

Max shrugged. "S'okay." Half of it was brown and purple, but it looked worse than it felt.

"Enough's enough, Max."

Max worried at his bottom lip, twisting the thick flesh between his front teeth.

"Three schools you've been through, and all of them you've been bullied. You can't keep swapping schools forever."

"I know."

"You're already behind in your schoolwork, and your teachers are all telling your mum that you're not pulling your weight in class."

"I know."

"You're going to throw your future away—"

"It's not my fault," Max protested. "I don't ask them to do it!"

"You're a target," Aunt Donna said firmly. "You don't stand up for yourself and—"

"He kicked me in the head!"

"For goodness' sake, Max, you're a big man! You—"

"Fatso Farrier, that's me."

"I said big, not fat," Aunt Donna returned. "You're tall and broad, the weight notwithstanding. Even if you lost it all and turned into an Olympic athlete, you'd still be a big man. You're like your father in that respect, and he wasn't fat by any means. And a big man like you—especially at your age, you'll probably get even bigger before you're through, I reckon you'll see six-foot easy—has no excuse for not even attempting to defend himself."

Max squirmed uncomfortably. "I don't like fighting," he mumbled.

"You don't have to like it, but you have to know how to do it." Aunt Donna swung the van off at the wrong exit from a roundabout, and Max frowned in confusion as they headed away from the shops and any errands he'd supposed she had to run. Brilliant. The 'errand' was a talking-to where Mum couldn't stick up for him, then.

"I can't fight."

"Everyone can learn how."

"Well, I can't."

"Yes, you bloody well will. You're letting smaller, cowardly little bastards beat you up for shits and giggles and not lifting a finger to defend yourself. It's not your fault they look to you in the first place, but you have a lot of control over whether they come back for seconds."

"But Mum says violence—"

"Your mum has had a nice, sheltered life where she's never been truly threatened." Her voice softened ever so slightly. "You and I know better, Max. Being a pacifist when someone's trying to kick your head in is just stupid. You have to know how to defend yourself."

"I could just fall on them," Max mumbled.

Aunt Donna snorted and swung the van into what looked like an old warehouse yard. Little brick-built units surrounded a central parking court, with a garage at one end belching heavy metal and the shrill sound of drilling into the sticky-hot air. A greasy-spoon cafe was at the other end, blocked in by other, dirtier work vans, and farting the greasy smell of beans and burnt sausages over the melting tarmac.

"Breakfast?" Max asked hopefully.

"You wish," Aunt Donna said. "Come on." She jumped down, light as anything, while Max tumbled, nearly stumbling to his knees as the heat assaulted him again. "I know the bloke who runs this place—his brother's a regular at the shop, television engineer or something like that…"

"Okay," Max said as Aunt Donna rummaged in the back of the van and chucked a rucksack at him. "What's that got to do with me?"

She just walked off. Kind of like the stalking around thing, that was Aunt Donna to a T, so Max shouldered the bag and followed her, thinking she was going to buy him a punching bag for the back garden or something stupid like that.

The unit Aunt Donna's mate's brother ran was between a building supplies business and a carpet fitters. It was barely a window and a door, paint peeling off the walls, and a damp little room beyond. Aunt Donna simply signed her name on a piece of paper on the unattended desk inside and stomped up a narrow flight of stairs into—

Shit.

Into a huge, cavernous space—obviously the top floor across all the units in this row. At the end of the unnecessarily large lobby area was a manned, tidy desk, with a long corridor of doors stretching out behind it. There was music, and the dank mix of sweat and Lynx deodorant, and—worst of all—posters upon posters on the walls.

Boxing competitions.

"No," he said to Aunt Donna.

A boy at the desk looked up at his voice, and a huge, ridiculously white smile bloomed across his thin face. He was tall and skinny, maybe twenty years old, with long dreadlocks and a face full of metal.

"Auntie Donna!" he crowed in a faint Caribbean accent, oddly mixed with Cornish. 'Auntie' was 'Anty,' but 'Donna' was dragged out longer in the South West fashion, and Max blinked, startled at the mix. "How you been, Auntie? You been avoiding the scene?"

"Just busy, Cal," Aunt Donna said, leaning over the desk to hug him briefly. "Got a wedding to plan, haven't I? Can't be playing the scene with seating arrangements in my head!"

"Ah, more fool you, Auntie Donna! Always play the scene," Cal returned jovially and then beamed at Max.

"Cal, this is my stepson, Max. I called Lewis about setting something up for him. Is he around?"

"Second bag room," Cal said, and Aunt Donna's hand clamped down like a claw on Max's shoulder. "He's with Cian on warm-up—I can hear the music. Just go right in. Pete has the main classes today."

"Special treatment for me, huh?" Aunt Donna shoved Max down the corridor. It was cooler there, but the music was louder—"Eye of the Tiger"—and there were no windows, giving it a slightly close, grim feel.

"I'm not boxing," Max said.

"No, you're not," Aunt Donna replied. "This is Muay Thai, not western boxing. Far more intensive as a workout, far more dangerous in a street fight."

"I'm not...Muay...Thai-ing either!"

"Yes, you bloody well are," Aunt Donna retorted. "I'm sick of watching you coming and going from school like someone's murdered your puppy every damn day, and I'm sick of your mum worrying and crying over it. You are perfectly capable of defending yourself, but you've let those bullies into your head. Your problem isn't that you're fat or you're out of shape, Max, it's your confidence. A kid who walks around like he owns the place doesn't get challenged nearly as much as the kid who hides in the shadows. You have a bullseye painted on your back, and Lewis can get rid of it."

"But I don't want to—"

"You want to get kicked in the head by that idiot Fallowfield lad instead, is that it?"

"No, but—"

"No buts. I've signed you up for sixteen weeks of—"

"Four months?!"

"—intensive, personal training with Lewis. It'll build your self-esteem and your confidence, and that's what you need, Max. End of story."

"And if I refuse to come?"

Aunt Donna folded her arms over her chest. "If you miss even two sessions of your sixteen-week course here—no job at the shop when your GCSEs are over."

Max paled. Aunt Donna worked in an independent electronics shop that offered electronics apprenticeships to any of the local teenagers who wanted to be a skivvy for shit pay. It was Max's ticket out of school—if he was on an apprenticeship, he wouldn't have to attend sixth form with Jazz and his cronies anymore.

"You wouldn't," he croaked.

"I would."

"But—but Aunt Donna—I'd have to—I'd have to go to school!"

"You'd have to face those idiots for two more years," Aunt Donna agreed. She stuck her chin out and raised her eyebrows. "So you can do that, with no tools to defend yourself, or you can do this and still have the chance to turn tail and run once you're sixteen. It's up to you."

Except it wasn't, because what kind of a horrible choice was that? Max stared at the floor, at his boat-like trainers, and scowled.

"Fine," he mumbled and pushed open the door behind which "Eye of the Tiger" had clicked over into a fast-paced version of "Bohemian Rhapsody."

Just in time to see a stocky black man in red boxing gloves smash his fist forward, and a skinny blond kid go crashing to the floor.

"Max," Aunt Donna said, "meet Lewis."

Chapter Two

"AND LEWIS, THIS is Max, my stepson."

The black man grinned. He was bouncing on the balls of his feet, gloved fists hovering around his waist, and he spoke thickly around a red gumshield. "Wi' you in a mirret, Dorra!"

The blond kid started to stagger drunkenly to his feet, looking a little dazed, and Lewis hooked an arm under his elbow and hauled.

"Orrite, Cian?"

The kid blinked and then nodded. With that, Lewis let go and stomped over the crash mats towards Max and Donna. He spat the gumshield into a plastic cup of water on a table by the door and began to unlace his gloves with his teeth.

"How's things, eh, Donna? Shop still going well? Heard you were getting married, you sneaky tart!"

"Can't play the scene forever, Lewis," Donna said and clapped Max on the shoulder. "This is Lucy's son."

Lewis squinted at Max and cocked his head. "One of the Farrier clan? Fuck me, must be, look at the shoulders on you, boy!" Unlike Cal at the desk, Lewis spoke with a Southampton accent, very quick and blurry. "And all that hair, looks like George Farrier before he fucked off to fuck his way around the Far East!"

"That's my uncle," Max said, unsure of quite how to respond to that. "Luke Farrier was my dad."

"Ah, sorry lad, shame what happened to Luke," Lewis said and then shrugged. "I didn't know him, like, but I've been around here long enough I remember them coming and going, whole clan of 'em, John and Mary Farrier's lads. Must've been most of the navy recruits from round here, Farriers!"

"Probably," Aunt Donna agreed. "Max needs some intensive training. Weight management secondary to confidence building, quite frankly. He's being bullied at school."

"Aunt Donna!" Max mumbled, going red.

"Been there," Lewis said cheerfully. "Cian! Cian, move your skinny arse over here!"

Max coloured as the skinny blond boy came over, and turned out to be a skinny blonde girl. Which was even worse. Max got embarrassed enough in PE in front of the other boys, but in front of the girls, it was just humiliating. Sweating in a tank top that showed off the fact he had the biggest breasts in the class was hardly the way to impress a girl.

Not that Cian seemed to really care. She just looked bored, shifting on her feet like she wanted to go and do laps around the mats or something.

"Muay Thai is about brute force," Lewis said, "and while someone outweighing you by a metric ton is going to be an issue, you're worse off if he's taller than heavier than you. And you and Cian are about the same height."

That much was true. Cian was a tall girl. She was maybe seventeen or so—Max had only started really growing properly last winter, so he was still lumbering along at five foot eight. But Cian was easily five seven herself, and most of it—

Muscle, actually. She looked boyish. Long limbs, wiry arms. Max could see the white strap of her sports bra under her tank top, and he shifted uncomfortably as his brain tried to mentally remove the top. Bad idea. No girl built like that, shifting from foot to foot and wearing a fat lip from her boxing instructor punching her in the face, was going to take his staring well.

He dropped his eyes to the floor instead and felt the sticky flush creeping up his neck.

"Cian's a lot lighter'n you are, but height's the important thing, and we don't want to beat the hell out of you just yet!" Lewis continued, and Max risked another glance upwards.

Lighter? No duh. Like, major understatement. For all she was tall, Cian was probably eight stone at the outside, and Max was sixteen. And at a second glance—the flush got worse, because once Max pushed past the lean muscle and awkward-looking gumshield—Cian was pretty. She was pale and freckly, with bright blue eyes and short-cropped hair the colour of wet sand. Rather than gloves, she wore strips of cloth around her palms and knuckles, and had long fingers but small hands when she stuck one out to shake Max's.

"Hi," Max mumbled, but Cian didn't say anything.

Great. Just great. Max had, to put it very bluntly, a thing for blue-eyed blondes. Learning to box with a nearly naked blue-eyed blonde was going to be torture. And constantly humiliating himself in front of her—

Yeah. This was going to be great for his confidence.

Thanks, Dr Donna.

"Honestly, Max, when your Donna here sounded out your situation to me, I thought immediately of our Cian. You've had your fair share of self-esteem issues and shitty kids at school, haven't you, Cian?"

That was met with silence and an epic eye-roll.

"Naff off, you little shit. Anyway. I figured best start you off quiet and private, like, with someone who's a bit sympathetic to where you are."

Max wanted to point out there was no way Cian had ever been fat, or even a bit chubby, but he held his tongue. Best not annoy the guy who beat up kids—Cian was sporting a bruise to match Max's black eye already—or the kid who was probably built out of steel ropes.

"Got a kit?"

Max blinked. "Um, what?"

"Have you got a kit?" Lewis repeated.

"In the bag," Aunt Donna said and smiled. "Have fun, Max. I'll pick you up in two hours."

"Two hours?" Max exclaimed.

"Hour and a half lesson, half an hour to mop yourself up in the changing rooms," Lewis said. "Cian, show him where the changing rooms are. And no fucking chocolate, or whatever else you've smuggled in. You need a protein shake, not a milkshake, you skinny little bastard."

Cian pulled a face that made her opinion of protein shakes abundantly clear, and jerked her head at Max.

"Aunt Donna!"

"Have fun," she repeated and shoved him after Cian into the lonely corridor.

Unsurprisingly, Cian didn't seem to want to talk to the lardy boy she was supposed to box with, and just walked down the corridor, opened another door, and nodded inside. Beyond was an empty room of lockers and a bank of showers—without any cubicles—at the far end, with a single toilet cubicle just visible in a corner. Thank God, no urinals.

"Do I have to shower before—?" Max started but turned to find Cian had already gone.

Faced with little choice—at least this evening, he could get Mum on her own and pester until she vetoed Aunt Donna's plan, because making a total tit of himself in front of classes of superfit boxing aficionados and pretty blonde girls was not Max's idea of how to boost his self-esteem, which thank you, Dr Donna, was not the problem!—Max opened the bag Aunt Donna had given him and squinted at the large shorts and tank top that awaited him. A tank top? Oh God, he was going to die. Or Cian was going to die, laughing herself to death at the idea of boxing with Max. God, this was going to be torture. This had to be illegal.

Still—given Aunt Donna's threat about the apprenticeship—it seemed he had no choice. Sighing, Max changed, the tank top clinging uncomfortably to his armpits and around his breasts. Cian was going to rupture something laughing; Max was sure of it.

"I hate you, Aunt Donna," Max told the rucksack and then edged out into the corridor. At least there was nobody else around. Boys' things filled the changing room, and he could hear a man barking orders in one of the other rooms, but—for now—there was nobody to witness his general grossness, except for Cian and Lewis.

Neither of whom so much as blinked when Max shuffled back into the chosen room. Cian was attacking one of the punching bags with suitably intimidating thwack noises every few seconds, and Lewis took Max to one side.

"Right," he said. "Warm up first—everyone does the same warm up as hard as they can—and then we'll get you started on the first few techniques."

Warm-up was just like PE at school: horrible, embarrassing, and totally pointless. At least Cian ignored him while Max wobbled and huffed his way through only four shuttle runs in the allocated time, failed to do even one sit-up, and managed a tremendously difficult two push-ups, biceps shaking. Lewis had to demonstrate what on earth a burpee was supposed to be, and doing squats just felt a little too like having serious constipation problems for Max's comfort. And then, once he was sweating buckets—and various folds he wasn't aware he even had had shaken themselves loose and joined in the sweating party—Lewis made him run five laps of the room.

"As long as it takes," he said.

'As long as it takes' took forever, and by the time Max heaved himself to a shaky halt, he was literally dripping and wanted to vomit. Cian just tossed him a pink hand towel and fetched a couple of bottles of water from a bag by the door, throwing one to Max—who missed and had to retrieve it—before uncapping the other and taking a long pull from it.

"That—was a warm—up?" Max gasped, towelling himself off. He felt as wet as if he'd taken a bath, and his knees were shaking.

"Hey, you put a lot of effort in, more than some of my customers," Lewis said, shrugging. "Cian, get Max a pair of gloves and help him put them on. And fetch a couple of training pads.

"Right, Max, footwork. Muay Thai is all about moving, you gotta keep moving in a fight. You stand still, you drop your weight down on your heels, and you're done for. So up on the balls of your feet, but keep your toes spread and flat. Look at my feet. Like that, yeah? Now shift your feet apart— you right-handed? Yeah? Okay, bring your left foot forward and just rock on your feet a little until you find a good solid balance."

"This feels dumb," Max admitted.

"Yeah, it looks pretty stupid when you're not doing nothing. But—" Lewis's hand lashed out and struck Max in the shoulder, his knuckles sinking into soft flesh and knocking Max effortlessly on his arse. "—that's what we're trying to avoid. You gotta have good balance, and your weight even and able to rock back to centre easy is how to do it."

The door banged as Cian returned, and Lewis beckoned her over.

"Fighting stance."

Instantly, Cian's languid, loose posture seized up. She rose up on the balls of her feet, heels leaving the floor and knees beginning to lightly rock as Lewis had shown Max. Her back and shoulders hunched too, her head shrinking down until her shoulders nearly touched her ears, and her hands, clenched into protective fists, came up to defend her face.

Max shifted, painfully aware he was only wearing some unforgiving shorts.

And so was Cian.

Shit.

"Now, Cian's a southpaw—sorry, a left-hander—so I want you to do the opposite," Lewis said. "See here where the left hand is near-touching the cheekbone? Your right hand needs to do that. And the other hovering in front of your eye a little further out—that's it. Your head is the most vulnerable part of you. Blows to the stomach, you can see them coming. Hitting the chest is a waste of time unless you're Bruce Banner. But the head is very vulnerable—very disorienting to be hit in the face, and it can end a fight in about half a second. Whatever you do, you do not drop this guard. Hit Cian."

"Um, what?"

"Hit Cian."

"What, just—?"

"In the face. Punch, slap, whatever you like. G'wan."

"Um," Max said, staring at his hand, and then balled it into a doughy fist and tentatively jabbed at Cian's face. Cian's nose wrinkled, her hand lashed out, and a sound slap was delivered to Max's wrist, pushing his hand away sharply. "Ow!"

"Hit proper, like you mean it. Cian's a right little knob sometimes, deserves it," Lewis said, and laughingly deflected a blow Cian aimed in his direction. "Sod off, Cian. The day you start sticking to your diet program is the day I stop calling you a prick in front of the newbies."

Max tried to hit her again and got another slap. The third time, Cian dropped back a couple of steps, rising and falling gently on her feet the whole time, and Lewis beamed.

"Now see, that's how to work your feet. Go on, Max, stay in reach. Keep rocking, keep your balance nice and even, don't overstep—that's it!"

It was like...a weird sort of dancing. Cian just bounced around all over the place, and Max was expected to keep up. At first, it felt stupid and clumsy, but the more Max moved around, his thighs slapping each other and Cian always just a little bit out of reach, the more natural it started to feel. Even if it fucking killed his ankles.

"All right, good, we got the hang of moving around," Lewis said. "Cian? Get the pads and glove up. Let's teach Max how to really hit someone."

Cian grinned this wide, toothy smile that turned her slightly bored face into something oddly manic. Max's gut twinged, and it wasn't from the workout.

"Finally," she said in a high, musical voice that went everywhere it wasn't supposed to on Max's body. "Now we're getting to the good stuff."

Chapter Three

MAX FELT LIKE he'd been crippled the next day.

Getting out of bed was nearly impossible. Everything between his scalp and his toes had locked up. The bruising on his face wasn't getting a look-in over the tight burn of pain when he so much as tried to wiggle his fingers. He'd never enjoyed a shower like he had that morning, and lifting his arms ached so much from the 'learning to hit proper' lesson that he had to get Mum to do his school tie for him.

And yet...

Weirdly, it felt...good. He kind of liked the burn. It was mad, given that it hurt, but...there was a little burst of satisfaction out of it every time he moved. Plus Mum told Aunt Donna to give him a lift to school.

"He worked so hard on Sunday, and his face is still all bruised up from that—that thug. Just drive him in, Donna. It won't take you out of your way."

Aunt Donna rolled her eyes but jerked her thumb at the door, and Max slid into the van grateful for the reprieve. It wasn't common for Jazz's lot to come and find him on the way to school, but it wasn't totally unheard of either, and right now, Max felt more unwieldy than ever.

"D'you reckon I'll be less stiff by next Sunday?" he asked as Aunt Donna started up the van.

"Next Sunday?" she asked. "You're going again this evening. Lewis is building it around that Ciara's—"

"Cian."

"—training—whatever—schedule. When she's free, you're free."

"But—!"

"I gave you your choice. You can drop out anytime, but it means school until you're eighteen."

Max subsided angrily. It really wasn't a choice. The only other way to get the apprenticeship would be to get into a college to do some shitty qualification in electronics or electronic engineering, and Max knew he would be up against way too much competition for it. Better to get the dogsbody job and do some training with Dave, the electrician who ran it.

"Why can't I just change schools?"

"Because it doesn't work, Max," Aunt Donna retorted, overtaking a Fiat Punto doing the speed limit, which, in Aunt Donna's eyes, was the equivalent of grandma driving. "You keep changing schools, and the problem follows you, if not the precise culprits. The Muay Thai will do you a lot of good."

"How d'you know?"

"For goodness' sake, you're not the only person who's ever been bullied," Aunt Donna said. "I was beaten up outside a gay bar with my first girlfriend when I was seventeen years old. Eight weeks in hospital, and nobody was ever convicted for it, because nobody cared to investigate or come forward to the police about it. It was just a couple of dykes. Nobody cared."

"But—"

"There will always be people who want to stomp on you. They don't care if you have the right to go about your life how you like; they don't care if you've ever done anything to them—they just find it funny. There will always be those people. And the best way of warding them off is letting them know you're not a victim, that picking on you is going to end very badly for them."

"By beating them up?"

"By defending yourself. Which means you stick this course at Muay Thai. I promise you, Max," Aunt Donna added as she pulled up outside the school, "that this'll change things."

Max doubted it as he hauled himself out of the van and dropped to the pavement. Aidan was a coward. But Jazz and Tom, not so much. Tom especially. And after Friday afternoon, Max was dreading seeing them.

Only...he didn't.

They usually waited by his locker for him in the mornings, but there was nobody there. He gathered his books hastily and cleared off, but when he lumbered into his form room for registration, there was no brooding scowl in the back row, flicking pen lids at the girls. Tom wasn't in.

Max began to feel sick. Had Tom been suspended? Or even expelled? He couldn't believe expelled. They hadn't expelled him for pushing Andy Simmons down the stairs at Christmas and breaking both his legs. But if he'd been suspended, then Jazz and Aidan were going to be furious. Tom was their favourite tool for beating up younger kids. He took all the flak from the school because he didn't give a shit, whereas Aidan's mum would leather him if he was suspended, and Jazz was too slippery to get blamed for anything. So if Tom had been suspended, then Max was so, so dead.

Not that his form room offered any protection. Nobody really talked to Max unless they had to—he was marked out by Jazz, like some kind of social leper. It was a dumb idea to be willing to socialise with somebody Jazz didn't like. The only upside of form room was that Jazz and Aidan were the year above and therefore not in it.

But Tom should have been.

Max twitched all the way through registration, eyes constantly flicking to the door, hoping for Tom to show up late. When he didn't, and the bell for first lessons rang, Max seized his bag and books with aggressive fervour. He had to get to his next class before Jazz and Aidan got to him.

Unfortunately, this school wasn't built for that.

Max had been through three schools since he was eleven, all because of bullying. And this one was not built for avoiding people—it was just one big building, with wide corridors and no back routes. There was only one way to get anywhere, and so it was speed, not stealth, that would let Max avoid anyone. But Max was too fat to be fast.

So he wasn't that surprised when, halfway between form room and his next class, a hand clamped down on his shoulder and drove him into a bank of lockers with a loud *clang*. He screwed up his face, held on to his books, and flinched back from Jazz's hot breath on his face.

"Why're you here, then?"

"History," Max squeaked.

"Oh right, yeah. 'Cause only, they were carrying on like Tom had done you in, and now you're swanning around here just fine."

Max wanted—desperately and stupidly—to point out the enormous bruise still swelling up his eye, and that it hurt to chew on one side. But he wasn't actually stupid, so he shrugged and edged towards the stairs.

"I have to get to History, Jazz..."

"Oh yeah?" Jazz's hand came up to casually flip Max's books out of his arms and onto the floor. They clattered around, one skidding off under the door to the girls' toilets, and Aidan cackled.

"Well, go and get it, Maximus Arse-us."

Max stooped to hastily gather what he could, before Jazz's shoe hit him square in the backside and propelled him—head first, again—into the toilets after the book.

"Hey! Get out!" a girl screeched, and Max seized the book and scrambled back out, face burning and sore, and stomach rolling in humiliation.

By the time he staggered to his feet, though, Jazz and Aidan had gone.

But Max knew the angry warning for what it was.

TOM HAD BEEN suspended, and Max was going to die.

The warning had been fairly clear, but it became downright obvious in his first lesson of the day, when Mrs Pellow simply bypassed Tom's name in the register like he didn't exist, like she knew he wouldn't be there, and why. Max sank a little lower in his seat when she did, and mentally wrote his last will and testament. Dead. So dead. When Tom Fallowfield came back to school, he and Jazz and Aidan were going to haul Max off into the toilets on the top floor that nobody used, and probably just kick him to death.

"All right, then," Mrs Pellow said, closing her folder and beaming around the room genially. She was in her forties, with floaty dark hair and glasses that magnified her eyes until every individual lash could be seen from the back of the classroom. "Today is for independent study on your chosen projects, as I told you last week. So I hope everyone's brought their research plans, notes, and a book or two to work from? I'll be coming round and talking to each of you in turn."

There was a general rustling and rumbling of mild dissent, but no real protest. History was a popular subject, largely because of Mrs Pellow's approach. Every term, she made them write an essay about anything they chose within the period of history the exam board were having them study, which this year was the Tudor period. Max had written an essay about developments in ballistics that made the British fleet more dangerous at sea.

Max kind of liked history—he could study what he wanted as well as what the exam board insisted—but he kind of didn't, too. Mrs Pellow wanted him to take the GCSE next year and the A-Level in sixth form. She said he had promise.

Well, what use was promise? Promise wouldn't get Jazz and his idiots off Max's back. Promise wouldn't get the Navy to accept a fat, useless lump in their ranks. Promise wasn't going to get him anywhere, and Max found the way Mrs Pellow would smile hopefully at him and say—

"Max, dear, how about you?"

He jumped violently, nearly sending his pencil case right off the table. He caught it just in time, flushing dully as she chuckled and crouched by his seat with her clipboard and notes, ready for the project he...

"Haven't started," he mumbled.

She blinked owlishly behind her glasses. "I see. Well, do you have any ideas?"

Max shrugged.

"Your paper last term showed great promi—"

"Yeah, well, promise isn't going to get me anywhere, is it?"

Mrs Pellow was very quiet for a minute before murmuring, "I heard what happened last week."

Max glanced inadvertently at Tom Fallowfield's empty desk. "What's that got to do with it?"

Mrs Pellow hummed. "Do your essay, Max. And take the A-Level next year—it'll be an easy grade for you, you're very good at history when you put your mind to it—and don't throw your future away because of boys like Tom."

Max bit his lip and stared down at his blank notebook.

"S'nothing to do with Tom," he said quietly. "There's just no point in my A-Levels. I'm going to get an apprentice at Aunt Donna's shop."

Mrs Pellow tutted and shook her head. "You're better than that, Max," she said. "You have real potential, you know. You just need to seize it."

Chapter Four

THE HOUSE WAS empty when Max got home.

It wasn't too surprising. Aunt Donna worked the shop all week and wasn't usually home until half five anyway (six if she took the bike) and Mum had a zero hours contract with a care home that was totally unpredictable. If they were out, they were out. And to an extent, Max preferred it that way. It gave him time to compose himself after school and not worry Mum.

Max dropped his school bag on the hall floor and headed straight for the kitchen. He took a six-pack of Pepsi from the fridge and couple of packets of ginger biscuits from the snack drawer before heading upstairs to his room, deciding to forgo the TV and just put a movie on in his room or something.

Max liked their new house. Well, it wasn't new—it was Aunt Donna's—but he and Mum had abandoned the flat and moved in two years ago. It was only three bedrooms, and one of them was actually the old airing cupboard after Aunt Donna had upgraded to a combi boiler and had had the massive hot water tank taken out. But it had a neat little garden out the back, and Max's room at the front of the house had a sloping ceiling, perfect for hanging his little model ships from.

And boy, did Max have a lot of model ships.

He used to make them—get those kits from toyshops and things—and sprawl out on the floor for days making tiny little replicas of the entire naval fleet, historic and modern. HMS *Enterprise* was cruising sedately towards his window, and HMS *Bulwark* was a blot of grey war machinery over his desk. By the door, he had older wooden ships from the Drake and Nelson eras, and he'd even mocked up a couple of models of his own when he was twelve, of the *Acheron* and *Surprise* from that Russell Crowe film. He had all the Patrick O'Brian books too. They were heavy going, but they were so cool with all the terminology and stuff. The guy had been a total naval history genius.

Max wanted to be in the navy, see.

Dad had been in the navy. And Grandpa Farrier too, so the sea was in Max's blood, and he'd give anything to be able to follow them. Grandpa Farrier had been in the war and then come home after—sans his left foot after an accident at sea—to marry Grandma and have five sons. John, Max, Luke, Tom, and George. All five had, like Grandpa, gone into the navy.

Uncle John was still in the navy, but nobody talked to him much because he was apparently a grumpy old fart, according to Mum. Uncle Max died before Max was even born, a climbing accident in the Alps while on shore leave. Luke was Max's dad—Luke and Lucy Farrier, which Max privately thought was a bad joke—and Uncle Tom was his twin. Uncle Tom still sent Max presents for his birthday and Christmas, and Skyped them from Australia sometimes. He worked out there with the Australian coastguard. And Uncle George…well, supposedly Uncle George was the stereotypical sailor, with a girl in every port, so Max probably had five billion cousins dotted around the globe by now.

But he didn't remember Dad.

Dad had died when Max was three. He'd collapsed ill on his ship and died about a fortnight later in Hong Kong from liver failure. Cancer. That was the dumbest part. He'd been in the navy; if he was supposed to die, it ought to have been drowning, really. But no: liver cancer. Max was three, Mum only eighteen and already widowed. Max barely remembered the funeral and didn't remember the man they'd buried at all.

It was cruel, in Max's opinion. He looked up to a memory other people had told him about. He couldn't even recall being upset about the loss. He'd been distraught when his grandfather died, but not his own father.

Grandpa Farrier had been a replacement, for a while. There'd been long evenings making model boats with him, even though Max had to do all the work because Grandpa's hands were arthritic and swollen. He took Max to see Grandma's grave every Sunday and told stories about all the things Max's dad and his uncles used to get up to, and how Grandma would wallop them with a big wooden spoon if they went too far. Grandpa used to take him to Portsmouth every month too, and whenever a big ship came in, he always dressed in his old uniform and all the people on the docks saluted him and made a fuss of Max like they were family or old friends. When Grandpa Farrier died, it was horrible. It was, Max imagined, like losing a father.

And ever since, there'd been this big hole of failure in his chest. Grandpa had been in his fifties before he and Grandma even had Uncle John, so he was super old by the time Max was born. He hadn't lived long enough to see Max go into the navy or even the cadets. Though maybe it was kinder that Grandpa had died before he could realise that Fatso Farrier was never going to join the navy.

Now he knew better, Max reflected morosely as he tore open the second packet of biscuits and made a start on that too. He was the end of the Farrier naval history. Grandpa was gone. Max was a fat, useless lump, and the most he was ever going to get out of life was being a general dogsbody at Aunt Donna's shop. He'd never get into the navy. He'd be lucky if he even got on a ferry for a trip to the Isle of Wight. His weight would probably sink the ship.

"Fatso Farrier," he told the first biscuit of the second packet and reached for the remote control.

What did it matter anyway?

AUNT DONNA GOT home at quarter to six, just as the movie was getting good, and frowned at Max from his bedroom doorway.

"I see you've already eaten," she said.

Max shrugged, dislodging the empty biscuit wrappers. There were crumbs stuck in his school collar, and his stomach sloshed uneasily with the six cans of Pepsi he'd drunk. He felt sweaty and uncomfortable, but it still didn't mean he wanted to move.

"Get your kit, then."

"What?"

"You've got training at the gym in forty minutes," Aunt Donna said.

"But—"

"We've discussed this."

Max sourly thought that Aunt Donna had discussed it, and he'd been strong-armed into doing what Aunt Donna wanted, but the raised eyebrow dared him to challenge her, and challenging Aunt Donna was about as stupid as challenging Jazz.

So he heaved himself off the bed and started fumbling for his kit. Sixteen weeks wasn't that long after all.

Thing was, usually, Max quite liked Aunt Donna. She wasn't really his aunt; she was Mum's fiancée. She was scary sharp, really fierce, and the kind of strong personality that Mum—who was super soft and caved easily—needed when people were trying to take advantage. And when she'd come along, Mum had gotten happy again, for the first time since Dad died. And Max loved his mum, he really did, and he figured at the time that if having Aunt Donna around was the price to pay for Mum being happy again, then he'd put up with it.

But then Aunt Donna helped him build his models and bought him new kits and, one birthday, bought him a sailing experience out on the English Channel. It had cost loads, and Mum insisted he was too young to start sailing or anything, but Aunt Donna just laughed and said, "Oh, he'll enjoy it, Lucy!" She turned out kind of cool, sometimes. So he did like Aunt Donna.

Just...not when she was turning that scary super sharpness on him.

She was like a bulldozer, and Max knew she wasn't totally above actually carrying out her threat, so he brushed the crumbs off and reached for his gym kit. Mum had washed it Sunday night, telling Aunt Donna off the whole time for making Max go, and it still smelled of fabric softener. It would smell of stinking gym soon, Max thought as he stuffed it into his bag.

Sweaty leather and cheap deodorant. He hated gym smells. He hated gyms in general—only the superfit went to gyms. Fat losers like Max weren't welcome there. People laughed at him, like when Mum had tried to persuade him to go to a swimming club because it would help him with the navy ambitions if he was a strong swimmer. The other boys had made jokes about Moby Dick and the great white whale, and they, of course, were all ridiculously fit and swimming for various school teams. This boxing stupidity wasn't going to be any different.

Except, something in the back of Max's head reminded him, it was just Lewis and Cian. Lewis wasn't allowed to laugh at him—he was the instructor—and Cian just...hadn't.

Lewis had said, Max reflected as he slowly began to gather his kit, that Cian had seen her fair share of shitty kids too. God only knew why. She was tall and pretty and obviously had an attitude, but...she hadn't talked much. Maybe she was socially awkward or something. Or maybe she was a pushover like Mum, or so prickly like Donna that she got people's backs up.

Max pondered it as he packed his kit bag and headed downstairs. Aunt Donna was standing in the narrow hall, sifting through the post with a bored air, and Max recalled her comment of having been bullied too. But now, nobody would have the balls to bully Aunt Donna. And Cian was a scary Muay Thai boxer fighter, so probably nobody'd bully her anymore. If Max got good at this Thai boxing thing, maybe he wouldn't be bullied either.

But Max's sceptical side pointed out that just meant kids at school might not bully him. Kids at the gym itself...

That was a different matter.

Chapter Five

THE GYM WAS busy this time.

There were loads of kids just milling about in the foyer—boys and girls, a cluster of little five-year-olds in tiny boxing gloves, and a larger group in their early twenties. Max hunched his shoulders against the looks thrown at him and had to barge his way through to the desk. Ears burning as he asked Cal where Lewis was, he was intensely grateful he'd changed at home.

"Same as last time," Cal said cheerily. "How's Auntie Donna, eh?"

"Fine," Max threw over his shoulder, unwilling to stay and talk with the staring crowd, and burst through the mayhem into the corridor. He took a moment to quietly hate Aunt Donna for making him do this, before pushing open the door to the training room.

It was empty. A single punching bag hung from a chain in the middle of the room, suspended from the exposed rafters. The radio on the windowsill was pumping out music again, and an open sports bag sat on the floor by the door with a towel and a three-quarters-full water bottle poking out of the top, but there was nobody around.

Max shrugged, dropped his bag, toed off his shoes, and lumbered onto the mat. Might as well get this torture over with. With that grim thought in mind, he began to jog around the mats in laps, huffing as his chest and stomach bounced and crushed the air from his lungs, his joints and muscles squealing in protest after the harsh treatment they'd had on Sunday. He'd just get it over with, put up with it, and then the minute sixteen weeks was over, go back to his room and stay there.

"You know," a voice said, "you're supposed to start with stretches."

Max's face burned hot.

"Um. Hi, Cian."

"Hey."

She was wearing a T-shirt today, those bra straps thankfully out of sight, but her bare feet were vulnerable and delicate as she padded across the mats. Max found himself staring at them. They were narrow, with high arches and tiny toes. He had a horrible, suicidal impulse to touch them.

"You okay?"

Max jumped. Cian was staring right back, eyebrow raised.

"Um. Yes. Yes. Um."

"Um-yes-um. Is that Latin?"

The heat in Max's face deepened, and she chuckled. It was oddly low. Sedate. Not the high giggle of other girls.

"Relax. I'm kidding. Max, wasn't it?"

"Y-yes."

"Don't let me stop you. Carry on with your warm-up."

How humiliating, to lumber off at a staggering jog again, especially when he turned to jog back and saw Cian practically doing the splits on the floor. Her shorts rose right up. Max could see the slightest curve of her inner thigh.

Oh God, he was going to die. He didn't have the energy for a sex drive and a sparring class.

Thankfully, the exhaustion soon overwhelmed him, and he glowered at the mats as he huffed and puffed his way through the laps, the godawful burpees, and the mountain climbers that threatened to throw his tank top over his head and flash his breasts at poor Cian. To his relief, she ignored him, carrying out her own warm-up without a word—until he dropped to the mats after the final lap, and she clicked her tongue.

"Uh-uh. Up. Lewis said I'm to show you the basic moves."

"He's—he's not joining us?"

"He's running late with one of his clients. He'll be here soon, and there'll be hell to pay if you don't know what a body kick is by then."

If Max had thought Sunday's jabs and crosses had been bad, kicks were even worse. No amount of fat in the world disguised the explosion of pain at shins colliding. The strain of his inner thighs—and the terror of flashing his junk by lifting his shin high enough to swipe at her ribs—threatened to take Max to the floor with every practice.

But worst of all was the push kick. Burying his foot against her flat stomach, feeling the rock-hard abs beneath the sole and the soft swell of breasts just above his toes...

The next one, he aimed too low and nearly kicked her in the crotch.

"Watch it!"

"S-sorry. Sorry. Just—just—"

"Need a breather?"

Maybe it was the exhaustion, but the filter that stopped Max from being flat out murdered by his tormentors failed, and his mouth blurted out what his brain had been thinking all along.

"No. You're just distracting."

Cian blinked and backed up. The guard stayed up. The constant movement on her feet didn't cease.

But the attack itself—the lesson—paused.

"I'm distracting?"

Max grimaced. "Sorry, sorry, no, you're—"

"How am I distracting?"

"It's nothing."

"Uh-uh, that sounded like something unfiltered for once."

"I—what?"

"Come off it, Max. You've been holding your tongue since you arrived yesterday. Spit it out."

"Um—"

"How am I distracting?"

"It's nothing—"

"You find me scary?"

"Well, yeah, but—"

"You busy wondering how me bouncing around is going to make you feel better about yourself?"

It was true, but the flash of arrogance was oddly calming, and Max frowned.

"You're not that—"

"You busy wanting to hit on me rather than hit me?"

The blow was sudden. Pain exploded up his shin, and Max was felled. Like a great oak tree chopped down, he crashed to the mats in a flailing mess of sweat, fat, and embarrassment.

And Cian stopped moving.

Squatted down on her heels.

Grinning.

The smile was devastating. The gleam of blue under that shorn crop of wet-sand hair was horribly beautiful. The hands hanging loose between her spread knees were taunting. And the way she bent forward meant Max could see a bra strap again.

He wanted, very much, to die.

"You into girls, Max?"

"I'm not perving on you! I swear!"

"You into girls?"

Max cringed. "I—yes."

"You into boys?"

The question jarred.

"I—what?"

"Are. You. Into. Boys."

"N-no."

"Then you can stop perving—"

"I'm not!"

"—because I'm not a girl."

What?

Max blinked.

There was sweat sitting on his skin. There was a stench rising from his tank top. There was music thudding through the wall from the class in the next room.

And Cian was squatting on her—his—her?—heels, saying—

"You—"

"I'm a boy. Cian is a boy's name."

"You—but—"

Cian's voice became very soft. Almost...threatening.

"If you ever call me anything but a boy, or he, or him, or call those facts into question, I'll hit you."

Scratch that. Threatening. Outright threatening.

"So don't fuck with me, Max. You calling me a girl hurts. So don't make me hurt you back, because this? This is nothing."

The door banged. Lewis hollered a greeting and a demand for them to stop sitting around.

Cian flashed a huge smile and stood up.

"We're not sitting around!" she—he—protested, turning on Lewis with a bounce and a cheery demeanour that chilled Max to the bone. "I kind of went a bit too hard with a shin strike, and Max fell over, that's all!"

Max didn't even hear Lewis's reply.

He just stared at Cian, the threat ringing in his ears.

He. He, he, he, he.

And yet, when Cian turned back and raised her—*his* fists, and started bouncing, ready...

Max's eyes still dragged down to the shift of muscles in lean thighs, and he stared.

That's a boy, he told himself.

But apparently his brain didn't damn well care.

Chapter Six

MUM PLANTED THE plate in front of Max and her hand on his forehead.

"You're not warm," she said and squinted at him. "Are you sure you're okay, sweetie?"

"He's fine, Lucy," Aunt Donna mumbled from the depths of her magazine. *Women's Fitness*. Go figure. "Probably had a tough session. Right, Max?"

"Well, I think you're pushing too hard," Mum sniped. "What if he gets hurt?"

"He won't get hurt; he's not going to be competing."

"Does Cian compete?" Max blurted out.

Donna lowered her magazine. "Eh?"

"Cian."

"Who's—"

"The—" Girl. Boy. "My sparring partner."

"Oh. Dunno. Don't know anything about her."

Her.

"What about Lewis?"

"Oh, he practically runs the place," Aunt Donna said, going back to her magazine. "His brother actually owns it, but he's usually on deployment."

Max looked up from his plate. "He's in the navy?"

"Mm."

"So...does Lewis compete?"

"He used to. Not anymore. He's older than he looks. He's got a few competitors in there—Lisa Mullins, his missus, she's a former British champion. He trained her."

"And now they're married?"

Aunt Donna snorted. "Lisa can handle him. And Lewis is a sucker for a strong woman."

"Donna!" Mum scolded.

"What? It's true!"

"We don't need that sort of gossip at the table," Mum said.

"If you want gossip, I know that Lewis—"

Mum gave her a withering look, and Aunt Donna subsided with a cackle.

Max, though, was still turning over Cian's sweetly spoken threat in his head.

"So if you know all about Lewis, why don't you know anything about Cian?"

Donna shrugged. "Why would I? Not Lewis's kid. And Lewis has four brothers. I'm not keeping track of that shit. Why, you taken a fancy?"

Max opened his mouth to tell her about the threat and then closed it. He...ought not to. Telling stories about a boy so girly he could be mistaken for a proper girl in his shorts and tank top probably wasn't a good idea. Aunt Donna would tell. And then Cian would find out and just outright murder Max.

"Ah. You have."

"I've not!" he protested.

"Uh-huh." Aunt Donna's smile was practically sinister. "Of course, I should have remembered. You carried a torch for that Lauren Baker when we tried to get you to go to swimming club. Blonde and blue-eyed. Like Cian."

Max coloured and said Cian was nothing like Lauren. But it was a lie, and he knew his face was giving it away.

"Donna, don't tease," Mum scolded as she patted Max's arm on the table. "I think it's lovely. Is she your age? Are you going to ask her out?"

Mum's automatic assumption that Cian was a girl made the hairs on the back of Max's neck stand up. If Cian was a boy, then—then he fancied a boy.

"Um, no. I mean, yeah, sh—my age. My age. But I'm not going to, um. Ask."

"Why not?" Mum's face twisted and Max's gut twinged. "It can't hurt to ask, sweetie. I'm sure she'd like you."

A vicious wave of fuck you rose up in Max's chest.

"Oh, right, yeah, she'd love to go out with a fat lump like me," he ground out, pushing back from the table. "I'm not hungry."

"Max!"

"I'm not hungry!" he shouted and stormed from the kitchen.

Only once he'd creaked his way up the stairs and slammed the door to his room so hard the ships rocked on the ceiling like sailing through a typhoon, did the flash of self-pity and anger ease.

He dropped onto the bed. It groaned under his bulk.

He'd said she. He'd slipped up. And if he did it in front of Cian, Cian would hurt him. And it *would* hurt; Max was sure of that.

Shit.

"He," Max mumbled to himself. "He, he, he."

He turned onto his back and opened the snack drawer.

"He," he told the biscuit tin. "She's a he. He."

If he had to go through four months of hell with a girly-looking boy, at least he could try to make it as painless as possible.

"FATSO FARRIER. WHAT you doing here, lard-arse?"

The drawling voice made Max's blood run cold, and he instinctively hunched his shoulders, as though he could magically disappear. The bus shelter was suddenly a trap. And he knew—from bitter experience—that the passers-by on the street would do nothing to help.

"Oi, you deaf? The crumbs clogged your ears?"

"Hi, Jazz," he mumbled into his chest as shadows filled the entrance to the glass shelter. When he glanced fractionally upwards, there were three sets of boots.

Including some tan Timberlands.

"Answer my question. What you doing here?"

"Waiting for a bus."

"No shit, Fatso. You taking the piss?"

"No, Jazz."

"You calling me thick?"

"No."

"'Cause it kinda sounds like you are. Like you think I can't work out that you're in a bus stop waiting for a bus."

"Didn't mean it like that, Jazz," Max mumbled, trying to shrink into his shirt. He was still in his uniform. The sticky cling of the collar was getting stickier and clingier by the second, and it was nothing to do with the heat.

"So let's try again. What you doing here?"

Max's brain worked frantically. He couldn't say he was going to the gym. He couldn't. They'd—they'd—

"See a friend," he mumbled.

"A friend? Yeah right. Like a lard-arse like you has friends. What friend?"

"Just—just a friend."

"What's their name?"

"Cian," Max blurted out.

"Cian?" Jazz sounded scornful. "Is that a boy or a girl?"

"A—a—" He. "A boy."

"A boy. So you was lying."

"I'm not lying!"

"You said you didn't have a boyfriend," Jazz said. "Or maybe you don't remember that, after Tom played football with your head. Do you remember him saying that, Aidan?"

"Yeah."

"What about you, Tom?"

The grunt sent a chill down Max's spine, and he glanced up the road, looking hopefully for the bus.

"Wouldn't bother, Fatso. You're not getting no bus."

"W-what d—"

"You got Tom suspended. Might still be expelled. And Tom's old man wasn't happy about that, was he, Tom?"

Another grunt.

"See, Tom was just having a bit of fun, and then you had to go and make it personal. It was a stupid accident. He didn't mean to kick you that hard."

Max's fingers started to shake on the books. He was going to be sick. He was going to—

"He means it now."

"No-no-no, Jazz—"

"Excuse me."

A hand grabbed his collar. Max's guts dissolved.

"I won't say anything! I'll tell them it was an accident. I'll—"

"Should've said that first, Farrier."

"Excuse me."

The hand pulled. Max dropped his books as he was heaved forward off the bench. A foot caught around his own so he staggered, fumbling, unable to shield his face—

"Jesus! You lot fucking deaf? Move!"

The shrill annoyance of the girl slashed through it. The hand was ripped away, and Max stumbled back against the glass. It shuddered alarmingly—and then someone said his name brightly and sat down on the bench beside him.

Cian.

Cian, in baggy combats and a grey tank top. The white straps of a sports bra were visible again, her—no, no, his breasts not so much as curving the soft cotton concealing them.

Wait.

How did a boy that skinny have—

"Do you mind? We're talking here," Jazz said.

Cian glanced up at him. Eyed him. Raked those sharp blue eyes from head to toe and back again.

Then leaned back on the bench and crossed he—his feet at the ankles.

"Yeah, well, now *I'm* talking here," he said.

"Fine by me," Aidan interrupted, grinning. "Wanna talk to someone more interesting than Fatso Farrier here?"

Cian barely glanced at him. "No, thanks."

Jazz seemed to catch on, though, and grinned.

"What's a pretty girl like you want with a fat lump like him?" he asked. "You local? I know a great place we can talk."

"No, thanks," Cian repeated. "I'm a lesbian."

Max blinked in confusion.

"You what?"

Cian shrugged, giving Jazz the obvious once-over again. "Well, I am *now*," she—he—she?—said slowly and then glanced up the road. "Oh, hey, Max, here's our bus. C'mon. Oh, Jamie sent me this great video, look, it's Lewis getting his arse handed to him at this charity fight a few years ago—"

Cian's chatter—rambling, constant, and seemingly effortless—rolled right over all four boys, and Max found himself being towed to the curb with iron-tight fingers around his fat wrist. His books had somehow ended up under Cian's arm.

And then the doors closed behind them, and there was a seat under his arse, and Max remembered how to breathe.

"Thanks. I think," he mumbled.

"You think?" Cian asked. "You were about to get your teeth smashed in."

"No. Thanks. I mean—I'd rather you hadn't seen it."

Because he was stupidly confused about whether Cian was a boy or a girl, but his brain apparently didn't actually care because all it could think about was that wet-sand hair inches from his face, and there was a skinny knee belonging to a pretty—girl? guy?—pressing up behind his own.

Max felt hot, sweaty, fat, and disgusting.

And completely, inappropriately turned on.

"I'm confused," he admitted.

"About what?"

"You."

"Me?"

"The—you're..."

He glanced to the side. Cian was simply watching him, eyebrows raised.

Waiting.

Dangerous.

"Doesn't matter," he mumbled, and Cian rolled his eyes.

"I take it they're the reason your Aunt Donna wants you training?"

"She's not my aunt," Max blurted out.

Cian cocked his head.

"She's my stepmum."

"Oh."

"My mum's partner," Max said and Cian made a noise of understanding. "She turned up when I was a kid, and I called her aunt for a bit because I didn't really get it, and it...stuck."

"Do you like her?"

"She's okay."

Cian hummed. "I have a stepdad, but he's just...Dad. I don't remember a time before him being around."

"How did you know he was your stepdad, then?" Max asked in confusion, and Cian smirked.

"You looking at me right now?"

"Um—"

"He's Lewis's brother?"

The light bulb clicked.

"Oh!"

"Theeere you go," Cian said.

Max glanced around the bus nervously. Their only company was the driver and a kid at the back staring blankly out of the window and listening to headphones that were blasting a tinny *boomph-boomph-boomph* into the air.

"Um, can I ask...?"

Cian shrugged.

"You said—you're a boy."

"Yeah."

"But you told Jazz you're a lesbian."

Cian snorted. "Right, yeah, because I'm going to waste honesty on that piece of shit. Or the time to explain."

The coarse tone was a surprise, and Max reeled back.

"If it helps," Cian said, pressing the bell as the bus joined the roundabout, "if I stripped naked, I would look like a girl. I have the plumbing. I have the letter *F* on my passport. But I'm not. And in ten years, twenty years, whenever, you would strip me naked and swear blind I'd never been anything but a boy."

It clicked.

So Max had been—sort of—right.

And sort of very wrong.

Chapter Seven

THE GYM WAS blessedly cool.

The training session was not.

Cian seemed to completely forget or ignore their conversation on the bus, and Lewis had them doing body kick after push kick after body kick, until Max's crotch was so sore he was semi-convinced he could solve this being-attracted-to-Cian thing just by cutting off his junk, and it would be painless.

By the end of the two hours, Max was shaking all over. He limped out of the changing rooms half an hour after going in, only to find Cian sitting on the bench in the foyer, draining a water bottle like his life depended on it.

"Wanna talk?" he asked and held out another towards Max.

"Um...okay."

Not really, but...

But Cian looked...great. His hair was wet and ruffled up in short, sharp spikes. He was wearing a T-shirt again and looked like...like a boy. Flat-chested. Wiry. The jeans—denim, but with combat-style cut and pockets—were seriously helping.

He looked like a boy.

Still, Max wanted to push his top up and have a look at the abs he'd felt through those kicks all session.

Cian looked like a boy, and Max still fancied him, and—okay, so Max wasn't bothered about the whole maybe-bisexual thing. His mum was bisexual, and his stepmum was a gold star lesbian or something, so who cared, but—

But...

But he also knew that under the jeans was—you know. Not—

How did this work? If he wanted Cian, and Cian said he was a boy but was physically a girl—what did that make Max?

"You can sit down," Cian said.

"Oh." Max sank into another chair. The tired leather squeaked and groaned under his weight, and he felt his face beginning to flush.

"Is this going to be a problem?" Cian asked.

"Um...is what going to be a—?"

"Me being trans."

It hung in the air between them.

"I—no," Max said. "No."

"You've been skirting round me."

"You did threaten to kick me every time I called you a girl."

"So don't call me a girl and I won't; it's not that hard."

"But earlier you said you were a lesbi—"

"Good God," Cian muttered. "Yes, because your dickhead mate—"

"He's not my mate!"

Max shouted it. It rang around the empty foyer. And then Cian sat back with a grin.

"See, there's someone in there," he said, gesturing vaguely at Max, "that I'd like to get to know. The guy who pulls faces at Lewis and mumbles that I'm a dick for throwing in a body kick when he expects a push kick and thinks I can't hear him."

For the umpteenth time, Max felt a heat rising in his neck and face.

"But that guy is buried under this—"

"Flab?"

The icy look Cian threw at him was withering, and Max shrank back in his chair a little.

"Fear," Cian said.

"Fear? I'm not afra—"

Cian snorted.

"Fine," Max ground out. "Maybe I am. But I have Tom Fallowfield on my arse, and—"

"And you're taller than him."

Max blinked. "Um, no, not the mouthy ones. Tom's the one who didn't say anything, the one with the boots. The tan boots."

"You were taller than all of them."

Max frowned. "No, I'm not."

"Yeah, you are," Cian persisted. "You only look shorter than Tim—"

"Tom."

"Whatever. You only look shorter because you hunch up. Your posture's awful."

The "Gee, thanks," escaped before Max could stop it, and Cian sniggered.

"See?" he said. "There's someone awesome in there. You need to let him breathe."

Max bit his lip, unsure of what to do with that declaration.

"And for the record," Cian added, leaning forward to prop his elbows on his knees, "I'm really not as prickly as I seem. But if you call me a girl, and you treat me like a girl, I'll not be nice about it. And for the next four months, you want me to be nice to you."

"Yeah," Max agreed.

"But if you want to ask questions, go ahead. Take the risk."

"The risk?"

"Well, some questions just aren't appropriate."

"Like what?"

"Like whether I have a dick."

Max's eyes flicked down to Cian's jeans before he could stop them, and Cian laughed.

"You like me?"

Max's face exploded in heat, and the next laugh was louder and slightly incredulous.

"Seriously?"

Max groaned and covered his face with both hands.

"You like me," Cian repeated, and when Max peeked, he was grinning. "Well. I'm flattered."

"I'm going to die now," Max said.

"Nah, you'll live." Cian chuckled and drained his water bottle. He got up off the bench, all long limbs and languid ease, and Max stared at the seeming shift from...

From boy to girl to boy to girl. Max's eyes couldn't grip onto one or the other. Sitting with his knees spread and draining that bottle, he'd been a boy. Tossing the bottle in the bin with long, delicate fingers, he was suddenly a girl with a stylishly short cut. Picking up his bag and slinging it over his back, he was a boy again.

Jazz had seen a girl at the bus stop, and Max had seen—

Cian.

"Do you mind?" he called after Cian, on a sudden, suicidal impulse. "That Jazz thought you were a girl, and you told him you were a lesbian?"

"Of course I mind," Cian said, glancing over his shoulder from the door.

Then he grinned. The twisted canine showed. Max's gut twisted, and his heart performed some kind of weird jump in his chest.

"But it's not like I need tossers like that to know their girls from their boys, is it?"

Then he was gone.

"BISEXUAL."

The word sounded strange on Max's tongue. Not wrong, but strange.

"I'm bisexual," he told the ships sailing across his ceiling.

Well, maybe.

He fancied Cian. That much was obvious. Despite Aunt Donna's intentions, Max fervently hoped he wouldn't get any fitter at boxing, because if he had the energy to get inappropriate wood, he would.

Pun intended.

"Bisexual," he tried again.

Max liked girls. He'd always liked girls. Never done anything about it—what girl would want Fatso Farrier slobbering all over her, after all—but he knew he liked them. Didn't have to have done anything about it to know that.

But boys?

Cian was a boy. He'd looked like a boy, sitting on the bench. Had a flattish chest and wiry arms. Wore boys' clothes, cut his hair like a boy. Kind of...talked like a boy, even though the voice wasn't a boy's.

And in those glimpses, when he looked like a boy, Max had still thought he looked kind of hot.

So he might fancy a boy, too.

Only, under the jeans there was still a—well, a girl. Wasn't there? So, did he fancy a boy? Or...

Downstairs, he heard Aunt Donna's van start coughing and then rattle away into the street. Figuring the coast was clear—no way was he letting Aunt Donna overhear this—Max heaved himself off the bed and limped downstairs.

"Hey, sweetie." Mum was up to her elbows in pizza dough. "Making your favourite," she enthused and winked at him. "Let's not tell Donna, eh? She won't be back 'til late. We'll wash up proper when we're done, and she'll be none the wiser."

Max grinned, sliding into one of the kitchen chairs. Favourite meant triple-meat feast pizza with extra cheese and garlic bread on the side. All home-made, because between Dad and Aunt Donna there'd been a period when Mum could barely afford to feed them, and pizza had been a huge special treat when she got extra hours at work.

Now it was a special treat for when Aunt Donna had been on at him about his weight.

"Something bothering you, sweetie?"

Max shrugged, content to just sit and watch. He'd sat and watched Mum cook for most of his life. She always looked pretty and happy in the kitchen, with all her hair piled up on top of her head and wearing something from her collection of aprons. She looked relaxed. Not like…

Max's earliest memories of his mum were her crying. Just—crying. The days Grandpa had had to come over and get Max ready for school, because Mum was too sad to get out of bed in the mornings. The week he'd had to go and live with Uncle Mike and Aunt Hannah in Exeter because Mum had gotten so bad she'd not bought any food at all, and Grandpa had had to break in because Max couldn't reach the handle to open the front door.

Those days. After Dad.

Then Mum started to get better, and Max knew his mum was okay if she was cooking. So he got into the habit of watching. And then Aunt Donna started coming round, and Mum kind of went wild in the kitchen, trying all these new things to impress this newcomer, and then the newcomer became 'Auntie Donna,' and Max caught them being disgusting at the oven that one time.

So he didn't worry about Mum anymore, not since cooking and Aunt Donna, but the habit had never really faded away. The kitchen was a happy place.

So it felt fitting to say, "Mum? Between you and me?"

"Secrets, sweetie?"

"Uh-huh."

"Is it about that boxing club?"

"Uh. Maybe."

She turned to glance at him. A stray curl was bouncing around by her cheek, flour white instead of its usual deep brown. "Do you not want to go? I told Donna this isn't the solution. It's not your fault those stupid boys have nothing better to do than—"

"It's not that," Max interrupted. "It's, um. Hypothetically to do with the gym."

Mum raised her eyebrows. "Hypothetically?"

"I...hypothetically like someone."

"That—Cian, was it?"

"The...person I like," Max said very slowly, "who may or may not have anything to do with the boxing club..."

Mum dragged out the chair opposite and sat down.

"I like them," Max said. "And I thought they were a girl, but...they said they're a boy. And sometimes they do look like a boy. And I...still like them."

"As in, you're attracted to them?"

"Yeah."

"Oh, honey, you know it doesn't matter to me who you like."

"No, I know that," Max said. "I mean…does that make me bisexual? If he's a—"

"Is he transgender?"

She said the word very softly. Gently. Almost like it was something secret and shy, not the flat, matter-of-fact way Cian had rolled 'trans' off his tongue.

"Yeah," Max said.

"And 'he' is definitely the right word?"

"Yeah. He, uh. He was pretty clear about that."

"But he still…looks feminine?"

"Sometimes," Max said. "I mean, I thought he was. It was only when he told me he wasn't and said—said that. I mean, he looks…boyish. But not."

"Okay," Mum said. "Well, I think it's up to you to decide what to call yourself. Does he like you back?"

Max snorted. "Come off it, Mum."

"I'm perfectly off it," she replied. "If he doesn't, he's not very clever, is he?"

Max shrugged awkwardly.

"If he's not interested in you, then it doesn't really matter to him what you call yourself, does it?" Mum asked finally, pushing herself up from the table and getting back to the dough. "If he is, and you decide to have a relationship with him, then maybe that's something you'd need to talk about. He might not like the idea of having a straight boyfriend, but then if you don't think bisexual fits you, that's up to you."

Max squirmed at the idea of being in a relationship with Cian. Yeah, right.

"What if Dad had been a woman? Like—a trans woman?"

Mum bit her lip.

"Would that make you a lesbian?"

"No," she said and then shrugged as if rolling the mention of his father off her shoulders. "Your father might have been my only man, but he wasn't the only man I ever liked, honey. You know why Donna hates my boss?"

"Because he makes you work Sundays when she's off?"

"Nope. I once admitted to having a tiny bit of a crush on him."

"Ew, Mum!"

"Oh grow up," she tittered. "He's sweet!"

"He's *old*. He could have gone out with Grandma."

"Mm, well, I'm a lady and he's a gentleman," she said, preening a little and scattering more flour over her hair. "So, no. Even if your father had been a woman, I'd still be bi. Maybe that's the way you need to look at things. Maybe this boy is the first boy you've ever liked, or maybe he'll be the only boy, and as—well, if—he becomes more masculine, your interest will stop."

Max chewed on his lip and pictured Cian in those jeans and nothing else. There was a sort of blank space across his chest, because he really was so wiry Max wasn't sure if he had breasts or if they were just, like, super-pecs or something...

And he shifted uncomfortably in his chair.

"Maybe I'm bisexual," he said.

Mum glanced over her shoulder again, and her face softened.

"You okay with that, honey?"

"Yeah," Max said slowly. "I think so."

What did it matter anyway? Bisexual, straight...hell, he could go right out the other side and end up gayer than a Middle Earth elf, and he'd still be in the same position. Because maybe he liked Cian, maybe he only liked girl-Cian, maybe he could fancy every blonde girl in the world—but it didn't matter.

None of them would ever fancy him.

Chapter Eight

CIAN TURNED UP in a skirt.

"Say a word, I'll smash your teeth down your neck," he snapped at Max before he'd even closed the training room door.

"Um. Wasn't going to," Max said warily.

"I hate visiting my nan," Cian snarled—and stripped.

"Oh," Max said.

And—

He ought to turn away, but—

Cian just...took off all his clothes. Right there in the training room. In front of Max.

Okay, not all of them. He was wearing briefs. And a...bandage thing around his chest. But everything else came off. The skirt. A pair of tights. The top that Max vaguely recognised as the brand of clothing designed to be acceptable to stuffy old relatives without actually being too offensively horrible to wear.

And then there was just miles of that pale, lightly freckled skin, and those abs, and—

The Muay Thai shorts were pulled up mile-long legs, and Max cleared his suddenly very dry throat.

"Um, shouldn't you...use the changing rooms?"

"No, thanks. I get yelled at in the girls' and side-eyed in the boys'."

"Um—but—"

"If you're that much of a prude, you can wait outside," Cian said and turned his back.

"Holy hell," Max mumbled, turning his own when the bandage thing was ripped off, and Cian's completely naked back was exposed to him. Which meant on the other side, there'd be...

Max hadn't warmed up yet. And the sudden tightness in his underwear said that his body was totally okay with that lapse.

"I'm going to start warming up," he said, his voice absurdly loud in the echoing room, and he broke into a desperate run for the other side of the mats.

"You're a wuss!" Cian shouted after him, but by the time Max had staggered to the end of the room and turned round, the sports bra strap flashed a brilliant white across the room, and an army green tank top had been slung over those abs.

"You're—cruel," Max puffed when he got back, and Cian snorted.

"Cruel would be training in my bra."

"You wouldn't."

"Would. Have. Don't tempt me. It's hot in here."

"About to get hotter!" Lewis boomed as he crashed through the door. "You two look far too composed. Ten for ten—go!"

Max hated ten for ten. It was all ten warm-up exercises, each done ten times. Ten laps on their own killed him. Add ten burpees, ten squats, ten jumping jacks, and all the other torture methods to that?

He scowled at Cian, who just flipped him off and started jogging.

"You're also too happy," Lewis proclaimed. "Cian, you're grading next week."

"Dad said—"

"Your dad's not here. And you don't need to start competing just because you hit advanced."

Max frowned as he turned at the end of the mats and started to lumber back.

"I'm not competing for the women's titles."

Ah.

"I'm not going to make you." Lewis's voice was even. "And if you can backchat me, you're not running fast enough. That's an extra five runs for the both of you."

Seriously? Max groaned. It would take him the whole session to finish just the warm-up at this rate.

"I need you advanced if you're going to do the instructor's course," Lewis continued blandly, leaning against the closed door. "You don't have to compete if you don't want."

"They'll ask why I'm instructing anyone if I've never fought."

"And then you can show them your elbow strike, and they'll shut up."

"What's—an—elbow—strike," Max heaved as he turned for his fifth shuttle run. Cian was jogging backwards, the bastard.

Lewis laughed. "All right. I guess that sorts today's lesson plan."

Cian's face lit up.

"Not you. You don't get to break the private clients."

"What if I—"

"Five more!"

"Cian," Max groaned. "Shut—up!"

Cian laughed but dutifully shut up, lowering his head, turning to run the right way round, and beginning to sprint.

The warm-up dragged the blood back out of inappropriate places, and by the time Max had finished the tenth push-up, his arms shaking like blancmange in an earthquake, the sweat was literally dripping off him and onto the mats.

Cian, wordlessly, chucked him that pink hand towel again.

"Okay," Lewis said, clapping his hands and wandering casually onto the mats. "Elbow strikes. Efficient. Painful. Good way to stop a fight before it even starts. What happens if you smash someone in the head, Max?"

The *thunk* of Tom's boot echoed dully in Max's memory.

"You knock 'em out."

"Sometimes. Probably not with an elbow strike. What if you don't?"

"Um. Still daze them?"

"Bingo." Lewis grinned. He looked manic, with that huge grin. "Put your left hand on your left shoulder and stick out your elbow for me."

Max blinked but obeyed.

"Feel that?" Lewis asked, slapping the jut of bone, albeit hidden and cushioned under a heavy layer of flab. "Felt a bit odd, that, didn't it? But didn't hurt, did it?"

"No," Max admitted.

"It'll hurt him. The elbow strike drives that point down your opponent's forehead, with all your body weight behind it. Hell of a hard blow, and nine times out of ten, you'll break the skin. And what do head wounds do?"

"Bleed?"

"Like a mother. Split his face open with one of those— fight's over. He won't be able to see a damn thing. And in a street fight, everyone else panics at the amount of blood."

"But—but won't it..."

"Anywhere else, it's nothing more than a sharp graze or a scratch. It only works so well because the skull is so close to the surface, there's nothing to protect it, and the skin gets ripped between bone and bone."

"Between fat and bone," Max said.

"Yeah, granted, you probably won't be splitting no skin right now."

Max stared at the casual...

What, acknowledgement? Acceptance?

No, he decided. It was more the bland shrug. The way Lewis had skated over it like...

Like who cared?

But he was fat. Everyone cared. It was shitty to be fat.

"But there's a trade-off," Lewis continued. "A good strike, you put your body weight behind. And this is one of the few moves where if you hit home, your weight is going to present Cian with a serious problem."

"How?"

"How much you weigh?"

Max coloured fiercely.

"Enough," he ground out.

"Yeah, but what? Fifteen, sixteen stone?"

"About that," he mumbled.

"Right. Now imagine fifteen, sixteen stone coming down on your face via a point that gets driven from your hairline to the bridge of your nose."

Max grimaced, and Lewis chuckled.

"Yeah. It's not pleasant. And between us, you know, it's a good one for self-defence if, hypothetically speaking, somebody's giving you some bother."

Max narrowed his eyes.

"Lot of mess, no major damage, nice and quick, and it'll make 'em think twice. You know. Hypothetically."

"Hypothetically," Max said and grinned. Oh, man. Imagine getting to smack Jazz with sixteen stone via a point.

"We're only going to practice today. Takes a little getting used to. And Cian has to get his fitness up. So I'm gonna show you how, Max, and we're going to put this little knobhead through his paces—"

"Hey!"

"Max, you're gonna practice a strike at him. Then he does a lap of the room. When he gets back, you do it with the other elbow. Fast as you can. And Cian, I mean that. None of this jogging shit, I want you to run."

The elbow strike was—weird. It involved rolling the entire arm until his forearm was parallel to his ear and then jamming the elbow down in a rapid crash onto Cian's—well, the foot of air in front of Cian's face.

It felt awkward. And weird. And kind of horrible, the way it scrunched Max's shoulder fat into his neck. But the downward swipe of his elbow, even over air, felt sudden and brutal. The way he could shove his shoulder forward and drive his weight behind the strike felt powerful. When he decided to jump forward a little, Lewis laughed and said he was getting into it.

"Good heavy strike, that. Now get the speed up. If he sees it coming, he'll get out of the way. Cian, start dodging it if you see it coming."

That was harder. Cian was quick. And yet—Max followed. The awkward footwork was starting to come naturally. His calves didn't hurt so bad when he tried to follow and swipe again. And when Cian ducked away, and Max's elbow bounced off his shoulder with a heavy thump, Max laughed in dizzy, strange delight.

"Fuck me, glad that wasn't my head," Cian said and then flashed a heart-stopping grin and turned to run down the mats.

Max paused, one meaty arm in the air, and swallowed against a sudden pressure in his throat.

"Max? You okay?"

"Uh. Just—just need a drink."

The cool bottle of water soothed the burning in his face, but his hands still shook slightly as he returned to the mats and got into stance. Max scowled at his fists. Great. Even exhausted, his body wanted to embarrass him. Bad enough Cian had guessed, but to prove it?

He clenched his fists tighter inside the wraps.

"Here he comes, Max. Nice and fast, now."

Right arm. Roll. Jump forward. And strike.

He jumped into it, crashing his weight behind the blow. The crunch of bone shuddered up his arm. His shoulder wobbled with the impact. His balance was thrown, and both of them crashed to the mats, Max winded, and Cian—

"Whoops," Lewis said.

Max's jaw sagged.

"Oh shit. Oh my God. Are you—"

"He's fine," Lewis said. "Come on, Cian, sit up and let me have a look."

"Can't," Cian mumbled. "Might be sick."

"Max, there's a bucket by the door of the lads' changing rooms. Can you pop and grab it for us."

Max heaved himself to his feet. He thought he might be sick too. His elbow was smeared in a bright pink graze, throbbing dully, and Cian's face—

Christ, his face.

The blood was everywhere. On the mats, on his top, running down his face and neck in thick, brilliant streaks. Max couldn't even see the cut; there was so much blood. He was lying limp as a ragdoll, his hair streaked pink where Lewis had pushed it out of the way to have a better look.

"Max? Bucket."

Max turned and jogged for the door. His heart was suddenly in his mouth. He'd—he'd just ripped Cian's face open. He'd need stitches. He'd have a concussion. Or worse.

What if—what if Max had fractured his skull? What if he'd proper busted him open? What if—

The bucket had a mop in it, but no water. Max abandoned the mop and jogged back with the bucket, the adrenaline overriding his exhaustion. When he crashed through the door, Cian was sitting up, loosely cross-legged, head bowed and Lewis's hand dark and firm on the back of his neck.

"Cheers. There we go, kid. Puke away," Lewis said, shoving the bucket between Cian's knees. Cian gripped it but didn't otherwise move. "Now that was a strike, Max. Lovely work."

"Is he—is he okay?"

To Max's surprise, Cian gave a silent thumbs up, and Lewis chuckled.

"He's got a hard head. Like I said, elbow strikes look a lot worse than they are. Think you've rattled his brain cells a little, but there's only three of them, so I'd not worry."

Cian said something very rude—and then finally hurled. Max grimaced at the painful sound.

"I'll excuse that on grounds of a concussion." Lewis shifted onto his knees and pulled a phone out of his pocket. Max shifted uncomfortably on his feet and then hunkered down to sit on the mat.

"Um. Sorry?" he offered.

"Don't be," came a mumbled reply. "Was a good—"

The second wave of retching cut it off, and Max winced.

"Hey Josh, bob down to the private room and scrape our Cian off the floor, would you? Elbow strike," Lewis said. "Yeah, reckon he's got a concussion. Might need a stitch or two, can't tell yet. What? Naw, keep an eye on him, and if he doesn't get any worse, I'll run him down later. Still got half an hour in here."

Max stared.

"You—you can't continue the session."

Lewis grinned as he hung up. "He can't. I just found a newbie with a heckuva good elbow strike, so of course I can."

"But—but he's—"

The door opened, and a man in his twenties with dreadlocks down to his backside marched in and, without so much as a greeting, hauled Cian to his feet, bucket and all.

"Trust you," the man said, and then—that was it. Cian was gone, and Lewis was standing up.

"Come on, then. Let's get a couple of pads and work on that technique. Excellent on the power, but you'll hurt your shoulder doing it like that."

"But—"

"Max. He'll be fine."

Max frowned, glancing at the door.

"Promise," Lewis added, oddly soft. "He's probably got a bit of a concussion because of the sheer force you just smashed into his head, but he'll be fine. Not the first, won't be the last."

"The blood..."

"Head wound. You came in a bit low, so I think you've broken his nose as well. He'll be back in a couple of days with a shiner, right as rain."

Max chewed on his lip.

"Hey." Lewis clapped him on the shoulder and shook him lightly. "So your Aunt Donna might have told me the incident that landed you in here."

"Oh."

"Yeah, oh. Now imagine who'd have ended up in that ambulance if you'd done that to him before he kicked you."

Max duly imagined.

Then squared his shoulders and nodded.

"Okay. So—what did I do wrong?"

Chapter Nine

CIAN WASN'T AT the next session.

Granted, it was the next day, but—Max still kind of expected him to be there.

"He's fine," Lewis said when he asked. "His mum threw a bit of a fit. She's none too keen on the boxing business."

"Mine either."

"Mums generally aren't," Lewis agreed and clapped the pads together. "Twenty jabs, twenty crosses. Get your shoulders nice and loose. You ready for a proper class?"

Max missed. "What?"

"A proper class."

"With—with other boys?"

"And girls. Yes."

"No."

Lewis shrugged. "Harder than that."

The lack of argument felt—odd. Missing. And Max found himself making the excuse even though Lewis hadn't pushed.

"They'll laugh at me."

"They won't."

"They stare when I arrive."

"Because they haven't seen you before. We have regulars just like any other gym."

"It's not."

"Then what do you think it is?"

"Because I'm fat."

"Big deal. Not everyone stares because you're fat."

"What would you—" Max started...and then stopped.

Because of course Lewis would get stared at sometimes round here. Of course he would. Not for fat, but...

He would.

"Yeah, what would I know," Lewis said and snorted. "I'm going to put that down to you're too busy punching to think. Mountain climbers, five minutes. Go!"

Max groaned but dropped to his knees and hauled himself into the *V*. He hated these. He always felt like he was suffocating in his T-shirt.

"Your strike yesterday was good. You put your weight into what you're doing. You try hard."

Max wanted to add that he was out of shape, overweight, and unable to do as much as three body kicks without stopping for a breather, but talking during mountain climbers just...wasn't possible.

"You're getting fitter already."

He wasn't.

"And it's not easy to catch Cian. That's his strength. He's not strong, but he's fast. You're the opposite. You'll be good for each other. He won't be able to really hurt you, not without a heckuva lot of effort on his part, and if you catch him, he'll go down. Hard. But you need to catch him first, and if you don't, he'll wear you out and bring you down that way instead."

Good for each other. Christ, what a joke.

"Listen."

Lewis's knees appeared at the corner of Max's vision as he squatted down beside his head.

"If Cian came into the class with you, so you had someone to pair up with for the whole session, would you consider it? And—stop."

Max fell out of the mountain climber and grasped greedily for the bottle of water Lewis held out for him.

"Why—do—you want me—to go?"

"Because you're good," Lewis said. "And because with the right training, with enough training, you could be up on the foyer wall."

Max frowned.

"You mean—compete?"

"Yeah. One day."

Max blinked.

"You could really be something, Max," Lewis said quietly, "and the only person standing in the way is you."

AUNT DONNA WAS late to pick him up.

Which meant Max waited in the foyer for nearly fifteen minutes, staring up at the pictures on the wall.

He'd never really looked—never wanted to—but something about the conviction in Lewis's voice made him stare.

The pictures were all at competitions. Sweaty men and women in bright shorts, beaming in fight rings, with belts and arms aloft. All fit. Ripped arms and bulging pecs and concrete stomachs. A woman with black braids, winning a semi-final with a huge smile on her face, had thighs that could have snapped a man's neck. A man who looked a whole lot like Lewis, white teeth glowing out of a bruised face, could have taken on a bus and won.

They were fit and powerful and gloriously, defiantly happy.

Deliriously happy, in Max's view.

And Lewis thought he could end up in those pictures?

Like hell he could. Max could never look like those people. Could never be like those people. They'd never been bullied at school, or moved from place to place to get rid of it only to find it again, or lost—

The unexpected swell in his chest hurt, and Max blinked back tears and ducked away, out the doors and down the fire escape to wait in the yard.

They'd never been failures. Disappointments. They were successful.

Fatso Farrier was never going to be one of them.

Chapter Ten

THAT WEEKEND, AUNT Donna's mum came to visit.

The bad part was that Max hated her. She insisted on him calling her Grandma Gracie (and what even was that? It sounded like something out of a Saturday morning kids' cartoon) and she'd said she was his grandma now, and the past was the past.

Apparently, she'd meant that not having a nana growing up was the past. But Max had taken it to mean Grandpa and Grandma weren't his anymore because Mum had moved on. He'd never forgiven the old witch for it and had steadfastly refused to accept her as a grandmother ever since.

The plus side was that Mum and Aunt Donna weren't exactly Grandma Gracie's biggest fans either, so when Aunt Donna knocked on his bedroom door on Saturday morning and said, "I rang Lewis. Josh is free to go through a fitness session with you," Max took the out and grabbed his kit.

"I still don't like this," he said, just to make things clear, as he clambered into the van.

"I know," Aunt Donna said, "but a couple of hours with Josh and then walking home is better than all morning with the Wicked Witch of the West."

"Why am I walking home?"

"The shop is tragically going to flood later."

Max squinted sceptically at the brilliantly blue, utterly cloudless sky. "There's nothing in the shop to flood it."

"No, but the laundrette next door might have an accident."

Max smirked, Lewis's words drifting back to him.

"Hypothetically," he said.

Aunt Donna grinned from under her shades. "Yes. Hypothetically. Not a word to your mum."

"What do I get if I don't tell her?"

"A tenner, and I won't ask where you spent it."

Which, in Aunt Donna speak, meant he could buy whatever snacks he wanted and not get any hassle for it.

"Deal."

The roads were busy—maybe the rest of the town had heard that Grandma Gracie was coming for a visit, too—and Max was nearly hanging out of the window to avoid sweating to death in the van. He'd never been relieved to reach the courtyard before and had to unstick his shorts from the leather seat.

"Be back before dinner, or Lucy'll go mad," Aunt Donna called. And then she was turning the van around and gone in a clatter of cogs and a belch of thick, stinking smoke.

"Try engine trouble," Max mumbled. "It'd be more convincing than a flood."

He peered up the fire escape and felt the battered tenner in his pocket. He could just...not go. It wasn't a training day. This wasn't part of his sixteen-week course. He could just...wander off.

But something drew him in anyway.

The foyer was quiet. Cal was on the phone and waved Max towards the training room with a big grin. The changing rooms were packed with bags and clothes, and music was bellowing out of the main class area. Max changed hurriedly, pulling his tank top down as far as it would go, and shuffled barefoot into the private training room, carefully winding the wraps around his hands in hopes of avoiding the smelly communal gloves.

And stopped.

Josh wasn't there.

But Cian was. Squaring off to a punching bag at the far end of the room and...murdering it.

Max winced.

"Um," he called. "Hi. Sorry. I thought—"

Cian dropped out of the stance and turned. Grinned.

"'Bout time. I was bored, so I let Josh off the hook. You wanna spar?"

Max coloured. "Uh."

Just him and Cian, alone, and sparring? Without a proper warm-up or anything? Oh yeah, no way that could go wrong.

"Come on." Cian put his fists up, still grinning. "Let's play pretend. I'm that gobshite from the bus stop, and you're Fatso Farrier who don't take no shit from nobody."

Max winced again.

"Doesn't," he said. Then: "Double negative." Then: "Anybody."

"Sorr-ee." Cian finally lowered his fists.

And came over to the edge of the mats.

From clear across the room, Max hadn't really seen it. But—wow. Cian's face was a mess. His nose was still swollen. The entire left side, from temple to jawline, was a mottled medley of colours—green, purple, black, and brown—and his eye barely opened on that side, a sliver of blue showing. A gash, maybe two inches long, split his forehead cleanly—a straight line in a dark red pen from his hairline to his eyebrow. A single white slip of tape held it together, seeming almost precarious and delicate over the damage.

"Oh shit," Max said.

"What?"

"Your face."

Cian grinned. "Beautiful, isn't it?"

"Uhh..."

"Come on, Max, it's not fun if you don't get a scar out of it."

"Should you be boxing when you look like that?" Max asked doubtfully.

"Eh, don't hit me in the face and we'll be fine," Cian said, shrugging. He bounced away across the mats, and Max hesitantly followed.

They did warm up, though only stretches and a few laps each, and then Cian rummaged some pads out of a cupboard and put Max through enough jab and crosses to make his arms hurt.

And then, when Max was sweaty and disgusting and his arms were shaking so hard that the fat wings could have lifted him off the ground, Cian said: "Lewis said he wants you to go to the proper class."

Max groaned and dropped his arms.

"Yeah."

"You don't want to?"

"No."

"Why?"

"Told him," Max said. "They'll laugh at me."

"Sure, but that's why you kick 'em hard as you can." Cian clapped the pads. "Hey, wanna do some push kicks?"

"No. I want to walk home after."

"That can be your cool-down. Oh, hey, tell you what. I'll show you how to grapple."

Max frowned suspiciously.

"What's grappling?"

"Like a prolonged hug where you can shake someone around by the neck."

A hug? Max blanched. Crush Cian into his flabby, sweaty folds?

"Um, no thanks."

"Why?"

"Too—gross."

Cian's face closed a little.

"You can't catch it, Max," he said sharply.

"Catch—what?"

"Trans. You won't turn into a girl if you freaking touch me."

Max felt the colour drain out of his face.

"What? No! That's not what I meant! I meant—I meant you won't want to be touching me. Not—like this."

"Like what?"

"All...sweaty. Gross."

"Hey, genius. See the pit stains? You're not the only one who's humming a bit right now."

"I just—don't want to," Max said.

Not only would that be gross for Cian, but Max was terrified, given their haphazard and half-arsed warm up, that his body would betray him. It had been doing it more and more lately, trying to get...um...interested during a training session.

Cian, though, wasn't buying it. He frowned and dropped out of his fighting stance entirely.

"Level with me, Max. Do you have an issue here?"

"With...?"

"Me."

"No," Max said.

"Then why do you stay a good five feet away from me all the time?"

"Um. You might hit me. You know, you're the scary boxer kid, and I'm—" Fatso Farrier.

"—the kid who smashed my face open on his elbow on his sixth try."

Max opened his mouth to refute that…and then closed it again.

"You got a problem training with a trans guy?"

"No!"

"Because if you do, say it. Lewis can train you on his own. Or Josh can. But I don't like this—"

"That's not it," Max insisted. "I don't—I don't care if you're trans." Except for the bit where he fancied Cian like mad and was possibly bisexual, but who really cared about that anyway when he was standing in a room with—

"Really convincing, that. I'm not delicate. I can take it if you do. Just don't screw around like thi—"

"I'm standing mostly naked in a room with someone I fancy, all right?" Max said loudly.

Cian's jaw clicked shut.

"And if—if I—lately…" Max ran both hands through his hair and sighed heavily. "Lately, all I do in training is stare at you, and if you actually start hugging me and touching my neck or whatever, it's going to get really weird really fast, and that's just—gross, nobody wants to have some fat disgusting slob—"

"You don't want to touch me because you might…what? Get hard?"

Max closed his eyes with a grimace.

"Yeah," he mumbled.

"And I can't touch you because it's disgusting?"

"Yeah."

"What is?"

"Me."

"You think you're disgusting?"

Max snorted and opened his eyes again to scowl at Cian.

"Get real. I'm gross. I don't even have ankles, and my calves just go straight into feet. These are triple-extra-large shorts, and they're cutting a groove into my gut. I haven't seen my feet without bending over for years. It doesn't matter who I fancy, nobody would ever want—"

"Weird," Cian interrupted in the softest voice Max had ever heard, "because I see a guy with shoulders like a rugby player and the kind of jaw that could cut glass."

Max frowned.

"You what?"

"I see someone with a mean right hook and an even meaner elbow strike," Cian continued, stepping carefully across the mats, toes flexing, bare and vulnerable. "I see someone who would rather roll his eyes and huff than admit something's funny or that he's kind of secretly proud of what he just did."

Then he was just sort of—there.

Right there. Like...breathing on Max's face, right there.

"When you strip away the self-loathing," Cian whispered, so soft that his voice barely existed in the space between their faces, "there's somebody beautiful. Right. Here."

The kiss was soft.

Sweet.

The gentlest clasp of lip to lip. A sense, rather than a sensation, of heat and hope.

And Cian's palm was smooth and cool on Max's bare neck. Touching him.

Just...touching him.

Max pulled back like he was moving through water. He stared and then slowly lifted his fingers to his lips.

"I—"

The oddest smile crossed Cian's features, and the hand on Max's neck squeezed lightly before falling away.

"Yeah, well." Cian's voice was a little hoarse. "You, uh. You don't kiss during grappling. Usually."

"I—" Max repeated.

"I'll leave you to it. Don't...don't forget to cool down."

And then Cian was gone. The door banged.

And Max stood in the middle of the mats, fingers on his lips, all alone but for the electric shocks fading away from where Cian's skin had met his own.

Chapter Eleven

"MAX? WHAT THE hell you still doing here, kid?"

Max blinked the sweat out of his eyes and glanced down at his hands.

Oh.

"Jesus, kid, when I said you could make the competition circuit one day, this isn't how you train for it," Lewis groused. He slapped his dry hand down on Max's sweat-soaked shoulder and steered him away from the bag. "Come on; let's get a first aid kit on them knuckles then call Donna to come and pick you up. Bad day?"

"Uh—"

"Come on, sit on the bench. Let's see."

Max's knuckles were split open, bleeding sluggishly, and he hadn't even noticed. He stared dumbly at them as his body slowly came back online. His biceps were tight and painful. His neck and shoulders ached, and his hands were twin balls of agony glued onto the ends of his arms.

And yet over all of it, there was a buzz on his mouth like some invisible bee where Cian had kissed him.

Cian had—

Max swallowed and said, "Cian and I had a bit of a row."

"That's when you hit *him*, not the bags," Lewis said, popping open a green first aid box. "He's a prickly little shit sometimes. Nobody'd blame you for hauling off and clocking him one."

"He's your nephew, isn't he?"

"And Josh is my brother, my flesh and blood, but he's a useless waste of space at the best of times." Lewis glanced up at Max's face. "This, ah. Wouldn't be anything to do with that torch you're carrying for Cian, would it?"

Max blanched, and Lewis shrugged.

"You wear your thoughts on your face, Max."

"He, um. He already knew. But. Yeah, it was...kind of about that."

"I don't want to know," Lewis said, "but I'll say this. He blows up fast, and like I said, he's prickly. But he's also easy-going. If you've had a bit of a bust-up, he won't remember by the morning."

Max had the distinct impression Lewis wouldn't be right about that one.

"Best act like you've forgotten too, eh?"

Then his hands were wrapped in gauze and sticky antiseptic cream, sharp and stinging, and Lewis was saying something about ringing Aunt Donna.

"I was going to walk home," Max said, and Lewis coughed a laugh.

"You've been in there beating up a punching bag for the better part of three hours, kid. You're not walking home on your own."

Three hours?

Max stared at his hands and slowly curled them into fists.

The pain beat against his shredded knuckles and still wasn't as loud as the buzzing on his lips.

THE FIRST THING Grandma Gracie said when Max got home was, "Oh dear."

And she wasn't looking at his hands.

"Oh dear, dearie," she repeated, peering at him over the top of her glasses. "Lucy, dear, you really ought to get him into Weight Watchers. There's a—"

"Grace!" Mum said, a look of outrage on her face.

Max simply stared at them. At his not-grandmother sitting at the kitchen table like she owned the place. At his mother's appalled face and her hands shaking around the kettle as she poured the witch another cup of tea.

"He's boxing several times a week." Aunt Donna edged around him in the hall and marched into the kitchen in her best obnoxious electrician impression. She opened the fridge hard enough to rattle the bottles in the door.

"Boxing," Grandma Gracie said with a wrinkle of her nose. "Brainless sort of sport if you ask me."

"Nobody asked you," Max said loudly.

Silence.

He felt a flush creeping up his face and neck and turned away from the stunned faces in the kitchen, forcing his aching legs to heave him up the stairs one painful step at a time.

"There, you see?" he heard Grandma Gracie say shrilly. "Loutish behaviour. You can't let it carry on, Lucy!"

"Max!"

Max stopped at the top of the stairs and glowered back down. He wasn't going to apologise. He wasn't.

Aunt Donna stood at the bottom, staring up at him.

Then she winked. Grinned. And proffered a thumbs up.

Nice one, she mouthed—and then she was gone again.

A tiny smile found its way onto Max's mouth, but he slammed his bedroom door anyway.

Just to make the point.

Chapter Twelve

MONDAY WAS TORTURE.

Sometimes the sessions changed times because Cian did something twice a week and at weekends that shifted occasionally. But whatever it was, it didn't affect Monday.

So Max knew—*knew* he'd be going boxing again after school.

He couldn't decide which would be worse: training with a mostly naked Cian again, or Cian deciding not to come anymore and just training with Lewis. As if Max's reaction was too awful for Cian to face.

Max hadn't meant to just stand there like a moron, but Cian wasn't supposed to have done that. He was supposed to be grossed out. Like everybody else. He wasn't supposed to want to touch Max, much less kiss him. And Max had been stunned. Nobody had ever kissed him before. Nobody had ever liked him before.

And then along came Cian.

Max blamed the distraction for what happened next.

He ducked out of history as quickly as possible so Mrs Pellow wouldn't try talking to him about his independent study project, and then he failed to keep going. Because leaving early meant getting to the gym and seeing Cian early.

But leaving late meant—

The hand slammed into the locker beside his head, and Aidan's high snigger came from somewhere behind his shoulder. The buzzing on Max's mouth stopped, nearly a full twenty-four hours after Cian left it there.

"Did you hear the news, Fatso?"

Jazz. Aidan. But when Max closed his locker with shaking fingers and turned, no Tom.

"No."

"No, sir."

Max said nothing and Jazz's lip curled.

"They booted Tom out. Because of you."

Max's gut clenched. Tom gone was good.

"He's kind of pissed off."

And bad. Really bad.

"So I suggest," Jazz crooned, pushing his face up close to Max's, "that you and your lezzer girlfriend watch your backs."

Max blinked.

Then—

"My what."

"You heard. You fucked with my mate, Fatso. Now we're gonna fuck with yours. Or just, you know. Fuck her."

Max opened his mouth.

And he didn't know where it came from, didn't know where the stupid, suicidal impulse came from, but—

"I didn't know you were gay, Jazz."

"You what?"

Jazz's face twisted in revulsion. And Max's mouth just kept running on ahead, like Cian on the mats, fast and flighty and unstoppable. Uncatchable.

"Cian's not a girl. But, you know, that's okay. If you're into boys."

Then Max saw stars and there was a ringing in his ears. The locker door was cold. His nose was warm and wet.

"Hey!"

A teacher's voice and a coughing laugh.

"Watch your fucking back, Farrier. You and that tranny lezzer bitch."

And then their shoes were running, squeaking on the tiles, and a hand was hard on Max's arm. Mr Dunstable from the English department.

"Come on," he said. "Head's office."

"No." Max shrugged off the arm and touched his nose. He blinked away the dancing spots. It didn't hurt that bad. Cian had done worse in class. "It's fine. Look, it's stopped bleeding already."

"Max—"

"I have to get to the gym," Max insisted and pulled away from Mr Dunstable entirely. "I'm going to be late if I don't go."

He had to tell Cian.

Whatever the hell else was going on, he had to tell Cian.

THEY DIDN'T GET to talk all class. Maybe it was Cian's intention, or maybe it was Lewis's, but the entire class was the bleep test. Max hated the bleep test. Especially when compared to super-fit Cian, he felt like a lumbering dinosaur. And he couldn't even get above level four.

"It's your baseline," Lewis said after the first one. "Every grading you do, you have to score higher. Cian, you're borderline. You need to be consistently above eleven point five."

Max was so winded they didn't talk between tests, yet the only thing ringing in his head was Jazz's threat.

He didn't know whether to believe it.

He hadn't really had anyone for them to go after before. But then the other kids avoided him as if they knew they'd become targets by association. So maybe they would.

Part of him was like: let them try it on. Cian was hard as nails. He'd kick them in the heads or something.

But the other part...

Come on. What kind of kid would kick someone in the head like a football in the middle of the school corridors and then be pissed he got expelled for it? Tom would do something really nasty; Max was sure of it.

So sure that he skipped the shower, rubbing himself down with his towel and cramming himself back into his clothes so he could hightail it back into the corridor and catch Cian coming out of the private room, still in his shorts but with his shoes on and a different T-shirt in place.

"Cian, I need to talk to you."

"Oh," Cian said and flushed a funny pink colour.

And then Jazz melted away.

And Max found his heart was back around his throat and his lips were buzzing again.

"Uh," he said.

Crap. Crap! He didn't need to get tongue-tied. This wasn't about—about them. It was about—

"Sorry."

Max blinked.

"What?"

"Sorry," Cian said again, and the pink was approaching a full-on red. "I shouldn't have—just, sorry. Forget about it."

Max swallowed.

"Forget it," Cian repeated and then started for the door.

"Wait!"

The cool air outside was a pleasant shock, and Max reeled for a moment after the sweaty changing rooms. He grabbed for Cian's elbow, the skin smooth and soft under his fingers, and then Cian was staring up at him, two steps down, with those blue eyes glittering black in the dark.

"It's—it's about—" Max said.

Then...

Oh, screw it.

His brain—or rather, his body—rearranged the priorities. Cian could kick people in the head without any boots to help him, and he could touch Fatso Farrier without wanting to throw up, and Max had just sort of frozen up and blanked out him.

"I didn't mean to," Max said.

"What?"

"To—just stand there. Like an idiot."

Cian's face crinkled up. "What?"

"After you kissed me."

It sounded alien and wrong. Like something other people could say, but not Fatso Farrier. Who the hell would kiss Fatso Farrier?

Well...this kid.

The train-in-my-bra guy. With hair the colour of wet sand. And legs that went on for miles. And tiny, delicate-looking feet.

"I didn't mean to freeze up like that."

"Yeah, well," Cian mumbled, tugging his arm free. "I shouldn't have done it. It won't happen again."

He turned to go, and Max just opened his mouth and puked words again. Like in the corridor. But—

Better words.

"What if I want it to happen again?"

Cian stopped.

Just stopped. Right there on the stairs, one hand on the railings. In his shorts and T-shirt and trainers, in the dark. Like it didn't matter it was dark and Aunt Donna's van was rumbling in the courtyard below.

He just stopped.

"It shouldn't," Cian said faintly.

"Why not?" Max asked.

"It just…shouldn't."

Of course it shouldn't. Pretty, skinny, head-kicking kids like Cian shouldn't want to kiss fat, disgusting blobs like Max. But…he had. And Max liked that he had.

Max shrugged. "Yeah, well. Still kind of want it to."

Cian's shoulders hunched and he shook his head.

"Sorry," he mumbled and then started down again, bouncing down the steps. The metal jarred under Max's body, and the sudden stab of pain in his chest was worse than anything Grandma Gracie could say or Jazz could do.

The air was too thin and Max gulped for it. Felt something burning behind his eyes.

Of course it shouldn't happen. Of course—

"Oh, fuck it."

The mumble was sudden, sharp, and…not Max's. And then the stairs were bouncing again and that cool hand was on his neck and—

Max leaned forward this time. Tried to catch that buzzing sensation on his mouth. Tried to find where it came from, and it came from Cian somehow. From chapped lips and spearmint and the oddest scent of woodsmoke clinging to his skin.

The metal bounced.

The buzzing stayed but the heat was gone.

"Told myself I'd never be this thick," Cian mumbled, looking anywhere but at Max. But then the dark gaze flickered upwards and Max's breath caught. "But you're kind of good at screwing with the defences, you know?"

"I am?"

A smile crooked the corner of Cian's mouth.

"Yeah. Add that to the list of things you just don't see."

Then he turned and went properly. Didn't run, just went. And disappeared into the dark courtyard like a ghost, leaving Max standing on the stairs with a thundering heart in his chest and something fierce and territorial lingering in his fingers.

He'd wanted to—grab.

He'd wanted to touch back. Not just kiss, but…hold on.

Hold.

He staggered down the steps and shuffled across the broken concrete to the van. Aunt Donna raised her eyebrows at him and Max shrugged.

"Don't you shrug at me," she said and grinned. "I think you've got something to be telling me and your mum."

"Yeah, well." Max heaved himself up into the passenger side. "When I know, you'll know."

Chapter Thirteen

HE DIDN'T REMEMBER about Jazz until after dinner.

Grandma Gracie had left while he was at school, and Aunt Donna and Mum were debating how to leave her out of the wedding invitations (Mum wanted subtle and delicately handled; Aunt Donna favoured telling her to piss off), so it just sort of slipped Max's mind.

What with that kiss and all.

But it came creeping back in after dinner when he was scratching out some answers on his geography homework so he wouldn't get into trouble for having not done it again. Because in geography, he had to sit right next to Tom Fallowfield. And now, an empty desk.

Jazz's threat came creeping back, and Max's fingers seized up around the pen.

He hadn't told Cian.

Shit.

He abandoned the homework and went back downstairs. The kitchen table was covered in a big sheet of paper, Mum and Aunt Donna bent over it and working out seating arrangements. Max shifted awkwardly from foot to foot before deciding it was probably best, given Mum's tendency to talk to the school and get him in worse trouble, to ask Aunt Donna on her own.

"Aunt Donna?"

"Mm?"

"The light's gone out in my room."

"Use the lamp, then. I'll sort it in the morning," she mumbled.

"The lamp's gone too."

She glanced up, frowning.

"Uh. I think a fuse blew."

"What, the whole top floor?"

"Um, no, just my room."

She raised her eyebrows. "There's no special fuse for your room, Max."

"Well—they don't work. And I need to do my homework."

"Do it down here."

"I'm nearly done. Can you just come and fix it," he demanded, losing patience, and she huffed.

"Jesus Christ. Fine."

She handed her pen to Mum and threw Max a sour look as she got her home toolkit out from under the sink. Max winced. Would she help now he'd managed to piss her off?

And she went from pissed off to downright angry when she got to the top of the stairs and saw his perfectly well-lit room.

"What are you playing at, Max?"

"I need to call Cian."

"You'll see him tomorrow, for God's—"

"It's urgent."

Aunt Donna snorted. "I am not playing silly buggers for teenage hormo—"

"It's urgent," Max repeated in a low, desperate voice. "Jazz—Jazz came up to me at the end of school today and said because I got his friend into trouble, he was gonna fuck up my friend. And he means Cian. I have to tell Cian."

Aunt Donna's face softened. Fractionally.

"What exactly did he say?"

"That. 'Cos they expelled Tom, he's going to take it out on Cian. They—they thought he was a girl, and they said they're going to fuck her up. Or just fuck her."

The expression hardened again, and Aunt Donna's lips thinned.

"Right," she said. "And you don't want your mum to know this because...?"

"She'll just tell the school and Jazz will find out I told her and then they'll—they'll really go after me and Cian. Not just threaten. I just need to tell him."

"I take it they know who Cian is?"

"They saw him. With me. At a bus stop. And he mouthed off to them a bit."

"Good for him," she muttered and then shrugged. "I haven't got a clue about his number, Max."

"But you know Lewis. Lewis would know."

"I—yes, all right. Hang on. Won't be able to get hold of Lewis, this time of night, but Cal might be around."

He hovered in the doorway of his room as she stomped back downstairs. He heard Mum call out, and Aunt Donna yell something about plugs. Then she came back up the stairs already on her phone.

"Cal? Yeah, I'm all right. Look, bit urgent, your Cian, you don't have his number, do you?"

Max shifted nervously from foot to foot.

"Yeah, that'll do. Cheers." There was a pause. Then Max's heart rose up in his chest when Aunt Donna's voice switched into her polite, almost mumsy tone. The one she used with teachers at school or that cute policewoman who'd been knocking on doors asking for witnesses last summer when there'd been that car crash at the end of the road.

Which meant not Lewis.

"Hello, Mrs Williams, I'm sorry to bother you at this time of night..."

Who the hell was Mrs Williams?

"My name's Donna Watts. My stepson"—Max grimaced—"trains with your son, Cian?"

She was talking to Cian's mum?

"Is Cian available, please?"

There was a short pause.

"Ah, I see. Well, I just wanted to let you know, our Max has been having some problems with some of the boys at school. Bullying and the like. And a threat was made this morning involving your son as well."

Another long pause. Max's palms were sweating, and he wiped them anxiously on his pyjama bottoms. Could he talk to Cian yet?

"Nothing particularly specific. There was an incident, and one of the boys got expelled. From what Max has told me, his friends have decided that a good way to get back at Max would be to target Cian."

Max strained to hear the reply, but Mrs Williams spoke softly, and he could barely hear a murmur.

"Of course. I'd be happy to do that. Tomorrow afternoon? No problem. See you then."

And then she hung up, and Max's jaw sagged.

"Where's Cian?" he demanded.

"He's at training. Mrs Williams is going to come up to the gym tomorrow at the end of your training session, and we're all going to have a talk about it."

Max's stomach clenched up tight.

"That's—that's it? What if they go after him tomorrow?"

"She says she'll keep an eye on him tomorrow so he doesn't run into anyone."

Max had the distinct feeling that Cian wouldn't like that but kept his mouth shut. Better he was annoyed with Max than he got a kicking from Tom Fallowfield.

Or worse.

"Do your homework, Max," she said, sliding her phone into her back pocket and picking up her toolkit again. "Nothing's going to happen tomorrow."

No. Not to Cian.

ACTUALLY, NOTHING HAPPENED to Max at school either.

It wasn't a hundred per cent surprising. Tuesdays were usually quiet, and he made a special effort not to go to his locker after school. Instead, he went straight from his last class to the car park and found Mum waiting rather than Aunt Donna.

"Graeme called in sick this morning," she said, apparently blissfully unaware of last night's dilemma. "Donna will pick you up from the gym. Unless—you know. You don't feel well or something."

"What?"

"If you don't feel right, honey, you don't have to go."

"Um. No, that's—that's okay. I'm fine. I should go."

She hummed, drumming her fingers on the steering wheel.

"I just don't think Donna's being fair to you," she said finally as they joined the main road. "She shouldn't be holding the apprenticeship over your head, and she shouldn't have a go at you about your weight all the time either. If you really hate it, sweetheart, you don't have to go. Okay?"

Max hesitated.

He should jump on the offering. Never have to jog down those mats and make a fool of himself again. Not have to wake up hurting in the morning. Not have to put his ear to the changing room doors to make sure nobody was inside to see his folds when he needed a shower after the class.

"It's okay," he said. "It's only 'til the autumn anyway."

Mum hummed again, clearly unconvinced.

"Anyway," Max said. "I'll—you know. I'll look better in your wedding pictures."

She scoffed.

"Honey, you're going to look wonderful in the wedding pictures, boxing or no boxing. None of that nonsense, please. You're just fine the way you are."

Except Grandma Gracie's 'oh dear' was ringing in Max's head, and he scowled at his boat-shoes in the footwell.

"Only I'm not, am I?" he spat. "I'm fat, Mum."

"There's nothing wrong with being—"

"Obese."

"Max!"

"I am!" he insisted. "I'm fat. Face it. I'm Fatso Farrier."

"Oh for goodness' sake. You're tall, Max. And you have big shoulders. And—"

"And I'm carrying a whole other me," he said. "I could lose five stone and still be fat."

"Now you're being silly. There's absolutely nothing wrong with you. You're the spit of your father, you know, and—"

"Yeah, who's dead because he was too fat."

The sudden silence in the car was angry. Hurt. And Max's insides squirmed.

"Sorry, Mum," he mumbled.

She didn't say anything.

"I didn't mean that," he tried again.

But she only sighed and said, "Yes, you did."

She didn't say anything else until they got to the gym, and then it was just a soft reminder that Aunt Donna would pick him up. Max felt sick as she drove away. He hadn't meant it. Dad had been big, yeah, all the Farriers were big, but...

But alcohol had killed him. Not being fat. Not being another Fatso Farrier.

And to just throw it in Mum's face like that…

Max texted her another apology as he lumbered up the stairs and then pushed it all to the back of his mind.

There were other boys in the changing rooms this time, so he shoved himself into his clothes as quickly as possible, ears burning at their mutters, and slunk back out to the training room.

Lewis and Cian were already there. Cian's face was still bruised, so they were set to legwork, and if Cian knew about the impending meeting between his mum and Max's Aunt Donna, then he didn't show any signs of it. He seemed to be more focused than usual—or he just didn't want to look Max in the eye, concentrating overzealously on their feet, hunching so far into his guard that Max had no hope of breaking it.

Then in the middle of the session, he said, "Grade with me."

"What?" Max said.

"Saturday. Grade with me."

"Are you kidding? You're like a black belt."

Cian coughed a laugh. "No such thing in Muay Thai."

"Fine, but you're insane."

"You all grade together. I just have to do more than you do."

"So the beginners grade with the superfit competitors?"

"Yep."

"That's insane."

"Saves time," Cian said, shrugging. "Grade with me."

"There'll—there'll be others there."

"Yeah. Six of us. Seven, if you come. And Danny's new too."

Max shook his head. No way. He wasn't going to be grading. What was the point? He was never going to—

"Can't compete if you don't grade!" Lewis called over the music. "If you can talk, you're not working hard enough. Five laps, both of you. Now!"

Max groaned and began to lumber, legs aching. Cian went for a full sprint, but Max couldn't hope to match it and let himself be lapped as his brain churned over the invitation. Lewis had said he was good at that elbow strike. And that he'd be good.

Lewis was an instructor. And he'd competed.

When they were allowed to get back to sparring, Max licked his lips and said, "Cian? Is Lewis—does he tell the truth about how good you are?"

"What, here?"

"Yeah. Like, does he say you're good to make you keep coming, or—?"

"Kind of? He'll never say you're bad or anything. But if he says you could compete, then he's not lying. Ever."

Max bit his lip.

Lewis had said Max could be on the wall. That the only person standing in his way was Max himself.

And that it would have been different, that day, if Max had known how to elbow strike Tom's face. That someone else might have ended up in that ambulance.

"Okay. I'll grade."

He lowered his guard a little too far.

And Cian's shin rammed into his ribs, knocking the air out of him and sending him crashing to the mats.

"Sloppy, Max! Cian, don't get smug. You missed about four opportunities before that one. Up! Come on, Max, up you get! Wipe that smug little smirk off his face!"

Max hauled.

"He's gonna grade!" Cian shouted. "Aren't you, Max? You're gonna grade Saturday, aren't you?"

Lewis grinned. And Cian looked so pleased. Proud.

So Max said, "Yeah," and figured he could regret it Saturday.

Chapter Fourteen

AUNT DONNA AND Mrs Williams were waiting in the foyer when the session was over.

Cian simply said, "Hi, Mum," and flopped down into one of the chairs like he knew it was coming. Max hovered nervously by the desk, surveying them all.

Mrs Williams was—

Not like her son. At all.

Oh, she had that wet-sand hair, thick and straight, just like Cian's. She had the same pale skin and light freckles. She had blue eyes—a darker blue, but still blue.

But Cian was all whipcord thin, wiry and made of something hard and unyielding, something tough and beaten into shape.

Mrs Williams was...soft.

Fat, Max's mind supplied.

And it was true. She was fat. She was tall—again like her son—but she was what Mum might have called matronly. Wearing dark blue leggings and a polo shirt, she was bursting out of every inch of them. A patterned overall was slung over her arm, like she'd come from some kind of work, and the crook of her elbow was a meaty place into which the fabric had been stuffed. The strap of her handbag was cutting a line between her breasts, almost disappearing. Her round face had nothing like Cian's angular jaw, and her eyes and smile cut grooves into the flesh.

But—

Happy grooves. There were no frown lines. Even without smiling, she was smiling. And she was pretty. Unmistakeably, undeniably pretty.

Max relaxed a little as she eyed him right back, and then a proper smile glimmered out of her peaceable face.

"You must be Max," she said.

Her voice was gentle and soft, higher even than Cian's, and he relaxed even further on hearing it. She was kind. Soft. Nice.

"Yeah," he mumbled, feeling sweaty and greasy under her appraisal.

She chuckled. "Oh, sit down, dear. You look exhausted. Cian, what've you been up to, eh?"

"Nothing Lewis didn't tell me to do," Cian said.

"I'm sure," his mother returned, and then her deep blue eyes were back on Max. "Your mum tells me—"

"Stepmum—" Aunt Donna said.

"—Aunt Donna," Max said at the exact same time.

Mrs Williams either didn't notice or didn't care and steamrollered right over the pair of them. "—that you've been having some bullying issues, and these lads have decided our Cian might be a good way to get at you?"

Max swallowed.

Cian apparently hadn't known. His eyes widened, and he shot an incredulous look at Max.

"Seriously?" he said. "That gobby one thinks he can pull one over on me?"

"It's not him you need to worry about," Max mumbled.

It wasn't. Cian could—would—kick Jazz into next year.

"Which one is it, then?"

"The one with the boots."

"Oh, right. Tim."

"Tom."

"Tim sounds better."

"Zip it," Mrs Williams trilled, and Cian rolled his eyes but closed his mouth. "Why is...Tom...?"

"Yeah."

"Why is he a problem?"

"He likes to kick people in the head. With his boots on," Max said.

"I see."

"He pushed a kid down the stairs last year and broke him. And he's shoved my head in urinals and—"

He said it too fast, too much, and shut his mouth.

"He's violent," Aunt Donna said. "He's been expelled from Max's school after the last incident, which landed Max in the hospital."

Mrs Williams' smile dimmed and then suddenly returned.

"We're not unfamiliar with such problems," she said tactfully, and Cian groaned.

"Mum."

"Cian's had his fair share," she continued, as though he'd never spoken. "Has there been anything specific said?"

Fuck her.

"No," Max said. "Not really."

Well, it wasn't really. It wasn't a threat—just the sort of generic stupid crap Jazz would come out with about any girl.

Only...

"Um."

Max glanced at Cian. Back at Cian's mum. At Aunt Donna. Could he say it? Could he just—

"Can I talk to Cian on our own?"

"You're hardly in a locked room, dear."

He flushed hotly but squared his shoulders and glanced at Cian, who shrugged and levered himself out of the chair like it was an effort. They crossed the room in step, slipped out onto the dark metal stairs, and closed the door behind them like it was a closet and a crowd was waiting inside.

"What?" Cian said.

"I might have let slip you're trans."

Cian frowned. "What, to Jazz?"

"Yeah. He said—he said he'd fuck you up, or fuck you, and I said that made him gay because you're a boy. Only you'd said you were a lesbian, so—"

"But you didn't say the T-word?"

"No."

"Reckon he's smart enough to figure it out?"

"Yeah," Max admitted. "He did—uh. Well. Said. You know—'tranny.' He's not totally thick. Aidan and Tom are, but not Jazz."

Cian shrugged. "Okay. Well. It's not exactly dead secret round our way. Some people know. Some people who've tried to give me shit for it know."

"Your mum knows though, right?"

Cian snorted. "Well, yeah."

"I don't know!"

"Yeah, she does. Is that it?"

"Well, yeah..."

"Good, it's cold."

Cian wandered back inside like nothing had happened, and Max followed. Aunt Donna and Mrs Williams were discussing the matter as though there'd been no interruption, and Cian collapsed back into his selected chair with a thump.

"I know what Tom looks like," he told his mother. "I'll just avoid him. No problem."

"If Tom wants to talk to you, he talks to you," Max said.

"Then I'll break his nose," Cian said, shrugging. "It'll be just like Ryan Cutter."

"Who?"

"This kid who tried to touch me up at school once. I broke his arm in three places."

"You also got suspended," Mrs Williams said dryly, but then she chuckled and looked at Aunt Donna. "I do appreciate the warning, but my brood tend to be a bit more...wildfire than your Max, I suspect. We tend to have a bit of a brutal approach to bullying."

Aunt Donna's mouth twitched. "Maybe Max could do with a bit of wildfire. He's a little too reluctant to engage."

"Cian could do with some reluctance now and then."

"Hey!" Cian objected.

"Don't make me tell them what happened in Year Seven," his mother warned and then rustled to her feet. Like Max, she had to haul herself upright. Unlike Max, she didn't seem to be in the least bit self-conscious about it. "Come on, dear. Time to get home. You know the bumblebees will be kicking up a fuss if they don't get fed and watered by seven."

She shepherded Cian out effortlessly, Cian waving a casual goodbye before starting to bend her ear about Saturday and someone called David, and then—just like that—they were gone.

"Bumblebees?" Aunt Donna asked.

"I don't know," Max mumbled.

"She seems nice."

"Um. Yeah? I guess?"

"Always good to have a nice mother-in-law."

"Aunt Donna!"

THAT NIGHT, MAX found himself going through the moves he knew in his head, one by one. Sweeps. Shin strikes. Body kicks. Push kicks. Always ending with that elbow strike. The devastating blow that could fell the enemy with one thump of bone and a whole lot of blood.

He cycled through them, always ending with that blow, over and over.

What if he did grade on Saturday?

It would be the first time he'd ever done anything like that. Over the years, Aunt Donna had signed him up for every sports club going, but he'd never achieved anything. He'd dropped out of swimming club before the team trials, too ashamed to show his bulk in public. He'd never even shown up at the football club. And his times at the athletics club had been so poor they'd never even recorded them. Why bother? Might as well have labelled him Last by Miles Max.

But he might grade on Saturday.

It seemed absurdly soon to Max. It had only been six weeks. But then he'd been going five times a week, minimum. And Lewis had said he ought to start the proper classes.

Staring up at the HMS *Bulwark* in the dark—the very first ship he and Grandpa had built, when Max had only been seven years old—Max felt a lump forming in his throat.

If he could do this, maybe...maybe he wasn't the failure of the family after all.

Maybe there was something Fatso Farrier could be good at.

"If I grade," he told the ship, "then—then I'll go to the proper class."

If.

"Promise, Grandpa."

The ship—and, of course, Grandpa—didn't reply.

Chapter Fifteen

MAX FIGURED OUT the next day that Cian didn't listen to his mum very much.

Because when he shuffled out of school expecting his afternoon to consist of going home, eating a couple of packets of biscuits in front of the telly, and getting the evening off from training as usual, he instead found Cian sitting on the wall opposite the main entrance.

"Hey," he said and grinned.

"What are you doing here?" Max demanded.

Cian shrugged. "Want to hang out?"

Max's eyes raked the crowd of school uniforms. "What if Jazz sees you!" he hissed.

"So what if he does," Cian said and slid off the wall. He was wearing military combat trousers and a tight white T-shirt that was...distracting. At best.

"Uh," Max said.

"So? Want to hang out? No training today."

"You always have training."

"Not today. Come out to play, Max!" he added in a sing-song voice, and thin fingers seized around Max's wrist, digging into the flesh. Max's arm sizzled. "Come on; let's go do something."

"Like what?" Max asked stupidly.

"I don't know. Anything. Cinema? There's some good stuff showing. Or bad stuff, if you want to make fun of it."

For some reason, with Cian's fingers wrapped around his wrist like that, Max's only objection was: "In my uniform?"

Cian laughed. "All right, fine. Your place first so I can ogle you while you change, and then we can go do something?"

The idea of anyone—least of all Cian—ogling him in a good way while he changed made Max's belly squirm. Not altogether unpleasantly.

"Okay," he heard himself saying.

And then Cian's hand was in his.

Max stared.

They were...holding hands. Cian's fingers were intertwined with his own. Long. Thin. Pale against his pink sausage-fingers. And then they squeezed, and Max's entire arm jumped as if he'd been electrocuted.

"You have to lead this train," Cian said, grinning. "I don't know where your house is."

"Uh—"

Usually, it was a bus ride away. Two miles, which was one point nine miles more than Max ever walked anywhere. But with Cian's hand in his...

"It's a long walk."

"It's a nice day," Cian countered.

His thumb was rubbing the side of Max's knuckle.

Max swallowed. His throat rasped.

"Yeah," he mumbled and started to walk.

Nobody looked twice. The tight T-shirt meant there was a sort of...bump on Cian's chest where Max imagined he had...uh. A chest. But nobody stared as they cut through the town centre, which meant they thought Cian was a girl, only—

Only he didn't look it.

He had biceps inching out of the tight sleeves. His hair was all sticking up and crazy like he'd washed it and just run a hand through it as a means of combing it. And he walked in long strides like Max's, fluid and idle.

Max's chest squeezed.

He looked like—he.

A boy.

Max was holding hands with a boy.

And he wanted to—

Well.

He wanted to do lots of things. Like...like kiss him. Or touch that little slip of skin that appeared between trousers and T-shirt occasionally. Or—and this one made Max's heart beat a little too out of control—put his mouth on the jut of hip that was pushing at the combats every time Cian's right leg was in front of the left.

There was a freckle there. On the hip bone. And Max wanted to touch it.

And—the stuff below it.

On someone who looked just like a boy, right at that moment, and Max still wanted to do it.

"I'm bisexual," he mumbled.

"What?" Cian asked, cutting off mid-flow about some story about his day.

Max's face flooded with heat despite the coolness of the trees as they entered the park. The shadowed paths and soft, salt-tinged breeze soothed every part of his skin except for the burning in his face and the electric hum where Cian's fingers touched his own.

"Nothing."

"You're bi?"

"Um. Yeah. Must be."

"Must be?"

Max huffed, blowing up into his hair in an attempt to stop flushing.

"You look like a boy right now," he told the air determinedly. "Really like a boy. And I still want to—do stuff. So. Yeah. Must be."

Cian said nothing.

Then he stopped walking, and Max was pulled to a stop by the iron grip on his hand. Another hand was pushing his shoulder, and there was tree bark at his back and grass under his shoes.

And then there were two hands on his neck and none in his hands.

Cian's body was long and firm as he moulded himself up against Max, all rough clothes and hard frame underneath.

But his lips were soft and sweet on Max's mouth and tasted like the sea. Salt and summer.

Max put his sweaty palms on Cian's trouser-clad hips—to dry them, just to dry them, nothing else—and...

Breathed.

Felt.

Basked.

The shade of the trees was cool.

Everything else burned.

"I DON'T THINK I should come in," Cian said.

They were standing outside Max's front door. His skin was going pink in the blazing sun. And that freckle on his hip wouldn't leave Max's mind.

"Why?" Max asked.

They were joined at the hands again, and Max's mouth was buzzing like they were still joined at the mouth in the shade of the trees.

"Because if I do," Cian said, "then you're going to get changed. And I'll be in the same room. And then I'll want to—do stuff."

Max licked his lips.

"We could do stuff," he said quietly.

Cian shook his head. "No. We couldn't."

He didn't want to ask. But he did want to ask. But—

"So—wait here?"

Cian wanted to hold his hand. Cian wanted to kiss him. Cian wanted—and didn't, at the same time, but still wanted—to do other stuff involving...being inside and Max getting changed.

It was all a bit dizzying, and Max's heart was pounding against his ribs harder than it did in the gym.

"Wait here?" he repeated. "I'll be quick. Promise."

Cian slowly stepped back. His fingers pulled free, in tiny tugs like they didn't want to slip free. Max swore he could feel the very whorls of fingerprints on his skin.

Then Cian pulled himself up on the gate and sat there. "Okay."

Max turned—and barrelled into the house.

He slammed the front door so hard he heard Mum yelp in the kitchen. He pounded up the stairs, dropping his bag, tie, and shoes on individual steps. He burst into his room with a speed he'd not managed since he was nine and shed the rest of his clothes across the carpet as he yanked open drawers for replacements. A black T-shirt was shoved over his head—maybe it would hide the pit stains from this oppressive summer—and he found his favourite jeans, designed in a combat style with additional pockets down the legs that went some way to disguising his bulk. The waistband felt loose, and he huffed before finding a belt. Mum must have stretched them in the wash or something.

"Max? Is that you?"

"Yeah, going out again, just getting changed!" he yelled.

"There's someone on the gate, darling!"

"It's Cian!"

"You can't leave him there!"

"We're going out!" he hollered as he found the new trainers Aunt Donna had bought him for Christmas. He'd not broken them to pieces under his weight yet, and they were stripey. Blue and white. Nice.

The front door opened again, and he heard Mum's soft voice rumbling gently. He paused a second to peer in the mirror, spiking up his hair with his hands hopefully before taking a deep breath.

Jesus.

He'd had to leave a boy outside because said boy would want to do things with him.

Sexy type things.

Jesus.

"You got this," Max told his reflection, for maybe the first time ever, and took another deep breath before walking out of his room, calm as though he did this every day.

Mum stared as he casually walked back downstairs. Cian, still sitting on the gate, beamed and gave him a very obvious once-over that made the now-loose jeans just a little bit tighter.

"Let's go," Max said, ignoring his mother.

"Oh, I see," Mum said, and he knew from the way she said it that she was smiling. "Well. Got your phone, dear?"

"Yeah."

"Have fun."

Then she shut the door behind him, and Cian laughed.

"Your mum's awesome."

Max shrugged. "Yeah, well. She's okay."

"She's awesome, man, no wonder she turned out you." Cian slid off the gate. He held out his hand again, fingers spread. Palm open.

Max wound their fingers together, tight and sure.

"Is this a—thing?" he asked.

"A thing?"

"A date-type thing."

"I don't know," Cian said, but the grin was taking up most of his face. "I think it's pretty clear I like you. I get the idea you like me. I guess it depends on what kind of film you want to see."

Max swallowed.

He shouldn't do it. Fatso Farriers didn't get the gir—guy.

Only—Cian was holding his hand. Had kissed him against a tree for thirteen whole minutes. Where anybody could see. Cian wanted him, however crazy it was.

"Something we've both seen before, or we don't actually want to see anyway," he said.

"Oh?"

"Yeah. You know. I won't be watching it anyway."

Cian's fingers squeezed tight.

"Then yeah," he said. "I guess this is a date-type thing."

Chapter Sixteen

HE HAD A boyfriend.

Fatso Farrier, the most pathetic lump west of Portsmouth, had a boyfriend. Was dating. Could change his Facebook status to 'in a relationship.'

Not that he would, because word would get back to Jazz and co., but still. He could have done.

He had a boyfriend.

And to top it off, his boyfriend was fit and funny and wanted to touch Max even when he was sweaty and shagged out at class.

Especially when he was sweaty and shagged out.

That sort of thing just didn't happen to people like Max. Nobody wanted their boyfriends to be fat, useless nobodies.

Only then Cian had said all that stuff when they'd first kissed, and for a brief moment—just a second, when he smiled—Max had believed him.

And every time Cian turned that smile on him or kissed him or twisted his fingers into Max's like they belonged there, Max believed him just a little bit more.

Which was why, when Mrs Pellow called him aside at the end of history on Friday afternoon and said, "Your form teacher says you haven't put your options forms in," Max—rather than walking out or making excuses—hesitated.

The options form.

A single sheet of paper on which he was supposed to list what courses he wanted to do in the sixth form. For the last two years of school he was desperate to get out of. For the last two years that would just be more torment by Jazz and his crew, and of no use to a nobody like Max anyway.

No.

He hadn't put it in.

Of course he hadn't. It was at home, sitting on the desk in his bedroom under a stack of other things he hadn't done. What did he want to do A-Levels and BTECs for? What use would they be to him behind the counter in Aunt Donna's shop, selling spark plugs and screwdrivers for the rest of his life?

Yet none of it came tripping off Max's tongue.

He opened his mouth and nothing came out at all.

"You're better than this, Max," Mrs Pellow said quietly. "You're smart. You've got the passion for it. Put your form in. Do something with your ability."

She sounded like Lewis.

"It doesn't matter if you don't know what you want to do yet—"

He was grading on Saturday. He had a boyfriend. And now Mrs Pellow wanted his options form, and Max couldn't find the words.

What was going on?

"Navy."

It slipped out. Just slithered out around his tongue like someone else had put it there.

Instantly, he recoiled. No. Stupid. A boyfriend and a boxing club didn't mean he was going to end up a bloody admiral. He was being ridiculous.

"Doesn't matter," he backtracked quickly. "Navy wouldn't want someone like me."

"Someone clever with a passion for naval history?" Mrs Pellow countered. "Someone who is deliberately failing geography because he sits next to Thomas Fallowfield and doesn't want to be an even bigger target than he already is?"

Max's head shot up to stare at her.

"We know, Max. You lot don't give us teachers enough credit."

"It—it doesn't matter—"

"Tom isn't here anymore," she said softly. "And you have a bright future ahead of you if you'd only grasp it. Put your form in."

Max dropped his head again and shrugged awkwardly.

"Don't want to do two more years."

"So to avoid it, you'll throw away university? A good career? An officer's position?"

Officer.

It rang over Max's skin, bright and gaudy. An officer. Like Dad. Like Grandpa.

He shook it off, an anger starting to bubble up in his chest. It wouldn't happen. No matter how many qualifications he had, the Navy didn't want shit from some fat lump like him.

"They wouldn't have me. And I've got Aunt Donna's shop."

"Your potential—"

"What good's potential when they wouldn't take me anyway?" he demanded.

"Why wouldn't they?"

Max felt his lip curl.

"Fatso Farrier."

She flinched.

"I'd sink a ship if I boarded it."

"Really." Her voice was suddenly wintry, and Max shivered as though the room had frozen over. "I think maybe it's time you had a good, long look in the mirror, Max. It's been dropping off you for weeks. And if you put the boy in that mirror to task, body and brain, the Navy would snatch you up and never let go."

Max scoffed at the floor. "What would you know?"

Silence. His palms felt slippery. His breathing was too fast. He'd never spoken back before. Not ever.

Then Mrs Pellow said, "Put your form in, Max."

"Can I go?"

She sighed. Heavily. Something like guilt twinged in Max's gut, but he didn't yield. What was the point? If he started dreaming about the Navy like he had before Grandpa had died, then he'd just be setting himself up to fail. Better not to cause himself any more grief than he already had to deal with.

After all, two more years of school, two more years of Jazz and Aidan and Tom, two more years of eating his lunch on the sly in the library to avoid them, two more years of constantly looking over his shoulder—and for what?

So the Navy could reject a fat, qualified loser instead of an unqualified one.

No.

"Go on, then."

Something like tears was blurring his vision, and something like shame was flooding his face with heat as he stumbled out of the classroom. The corridors were quiet. Mostly empty. He'd be late. Aunt Donna would be waiting.

He scrubbed at his eyes as he reached the bottom of the stairs—and so he never saw the boot.

But he felt it.

He tripped on it and went crashing to the floor. His phone flew out of his blazer pocket and skidded across the tiles. The crunch of glass, the squeak of rubber, said where it had landed.

And the voice cut through the heat in his head like an ice pick.

"You're late, Fatso."

The guilt and shame turned to anger, and Max shoved himself to his feet. He kicked at the shoe, too, and retrieved the battered phone.

"Whoa! Hold your horses, Fatso, I'm talking to you!"

A hand grabbed at his shoulder, but he shrugged it off and ploughed for the end of the corridor. Screw the locker. He'd just get yelled at for not turning in his homework next week. What did it matter? It never mattered.

The hand came back. His shoes squealed on the floor. The crunch of metal in his back was jarring.

And the fist in his gut doubled him up.

"I said," Jazz hissed in his ear, hot and fetid, "that I'm talking to you."

Max coughed, burbling uselessly.

"Say you're sorry."

His guts rolled. Jazz's elbow hooked under his neck, the point nudging Max's throat.

And Max sealed his lips shut.

"Say you're fucking sorry, Fatso."

No.

It was an insidious little whisper in the back of his head. And it sounded like Cian. No. Why should he? Mrs Pellow had no business telling him to put up with this for two more years. And Jazz had no business doing it.

"Fine." The sneer deepened. "Guess we'll have to teach you some manners."

Max braced.

And—

Pain.

It exploded through his groin, and he dropped with a strangled cough. The elbow scraped his throat. Dizzying. Dangerous. The knee hit his face then. Bone crunched, hot and wet inside somewhere. Then—

Temple.

Both sides. A bone on one. Metal on the other. A deafening bang as his skull was smashed between leg and locker, again and again and again.

From very far away, he could hear Jazz shouting.

"You think you're fucking better than me, Fatso? Do you? Do you?"

There was blood in his mouth. Thick and stringy. He tasted iron.

"You're nothing, Fatso Farrier. You're fucking nothing."

Max—blinked.

There was a ringing in his ears, but the banging had stopped. There was a puddle of foamy, pink-tinged sick on the floor between his shaking hands. He was kneeling. All fours. Like a dog.

And there were shoes on the other side of the sick, and a smirk.

Jazz was squatting down to smirk at him, and one of the shoes was bloodied.

"Tom says hi," Jazz breathed.

Max blinked again, but the image stayed the same.

"Do that again, and next time I won't stop when you piss yourself. Got it, Fatso?"

Max nodded. His vision danced. The corridor swirled. So did his stomach.

"You know what happens to snitches, Fatso?"

Very carefully, Max shook his head.

"Snitches get stitches. You got me? Snitches. Get. Stitches."

He was going to hurl.

"What happened here?"

The question was dangerously soft. And Max knew the answer off by heart.

"I tripped."

"And?"

"Banged my head."

"And?"

"Nothing."

"Good. 'Cause if it's something, something else will happen to your dyke bitch too. Got it?"

Max opened his mouth and spat. A glob of bloody sputum hit the floor.

"I'll take that as a yes."

Shoes squeaked. The spit floated in the sick, bobbing like a little bloody boat.

When the doors at the end of the corridor opened and closed, Max pushed himself to his feet. Swaying. Shaking. The soaked front of his trousers clung, heavy and clammy. His skin felt cold too. Sweaty. His hands scrabbled for purchase on the lockers, and he closed his eyes for a long minute to prevent himself from throwing up.

The corridor was still tinged pink. Everything was pink.

And—and if he said anything—

Cian.

He was going to be late for training.

When Max finally shuffled out to Aunt Donna's idling van, he'd catalogued it all. Broken nose. Bruises. Cut head. He'd match Cian after Max had clobbered him in class.

Only that had been an—

"What the hell happened?" Aunt Donna demanded.

"Accident."

She frowned. "What?"

"Tripped."

"And?"

"Banged my head."

"And?"

"Nothing."

Chapter Seventeen

MUM WAS CRYING.

Max could hear her from his room. Her and Aunt Donna arguing about what to do, and crying. Well, Mum. Aunt Donna was just swearing.

And Max felt—

Angry.

Mum would ignore him and Aunt Donna, tell the school, and Jazz would beat him up again for snitching. If he said nothing, Jazz would just keep doing it. And if he ratted Jazz out, Jazz would keep doing it anyway, because school wouldn't stop him.

And Max hadn't stopped him.

All Aunt Donna's plans about boxing helping hadn't done anything. He'd just let Jazz do it, because Fatso Farrier couldn't even defend himself.

"Well, we'll have to find somewhere else," Mum shouted downstairs.

Max scowled at his ships and muttered, "There *is* nowhere else," in time with Aunt Donna's bellowed reply.

He knew how this would go. More crying. More arguing. Aunt Donna would suggest something else—tennis, karate, whatever—and Mum would shout that he wasn't fat. He was just growing. Aunt Donna would shout, "Sideways!" And then Mum would scream that he wasn't Donna's son, and everything would go quiet before Aunt Donna stormed out.

Max was tired of it.

He was fat. He was pathetic. No amount of boxing or swimming or bloody Weight Watchers was going to change that. And no amount of talking to the school or moving around was ever going to get the target off his back rolls.

Suddenly he didn't want to hear it.

The bed creaked as he heaved himself free. The rowing downstairs was so loud that, for the first time, he was able to shuffle down to the hall, shove his feet into his shoes, and slip outside without being caught.

Then he stood in the warm, dark night, face and head still aching, alone.

Now what?

IT WAS GONE nine when he got to the gym.

The last class was clearing out, and Max hovered by the courtyard gates, watching them. He'd walked up on a whim. He didn't know if—

There.

It was the flash of fair hair that caught his eye, as Cian jogged down the stairs, weaving between the other boxers.

Max crept forward into the crack-pitted yard and yelled his name.

The rush of heat up his neck as everyone paused to stare—this fat intruder in a super-fit world—was bad. But the way Cian's face changed when he smiled made the heat go away.

Well, not away. Just south.

"Hey," Cian said, jogging over. "Lewis said you cancelled, and you're not grading tomorrow. Is your face something to do with that?"

"Yeah, something," Max said. "I tripped."

"Uh-huh."

Max rolled his eyes. Why bother? Cian kicked people in the head for sport. Like Jazz, but generally without his shoes on. And at least Cian only did it in the gym with people who'd given permission on the insurance forms.

Probably.

"Fine. Jazz kicked me. A lot. And I let him."

"Oh, right. FYI, not my kink."

The casual joke caught Max off guard, and he barked a stunned laugh.

"Did you kick him back?"

The laugh faded.

"No. Just fucking let him. Boxing's not doing shit. I'm gonna quit." Mum had said he could, before this. She'd definitely let him now, and not let Aunt Donna punish him for it.

"You're not allowed to quit."

"Yeah, well, Mum's not going to let Aunt Donna make me come anymore, not no—hey!"

The slap flashed out of nowhere. The crack of Max's palm, smashing Cian's hand away before it could make contact, was loud in the gloom.

And Cian smiled.

"It's working fine. Come anyway."

Max frowned.

"I didn't defend myself against Jazz." He looked at his own hand like it didn't belong to him. He hadn't thought about the parry. He'd just...done it.

"You're scared of him."

Max opened his mouth to deny it—and then closed it again. What was the point? He was. Everybody knew it.

Including Jazz.

"Keep coming," Cian said softly and then smirked again. "If you don't, that's one hundred percent less sweaty semi-nudity in your life. And mine. Not cool."

Max huffed another laugh, feeling the heat starting to creep back up his neck but with an entirely different sensation.

"Speaking of nudity—" Cian's fingers caught at his own. "Coming over?"

Max swallowed nervously. Go to Cian's? To do—stuff? Like...?

"Er..."

"I'll take that as a yes," Cian said and pulled.

Chapter Eighteen

CIAN LIVED AT the top of the hill.

It explained the rock-hard lines of his calves, Max decided, as they finally came over the crest into a nest of hedgerows and old cottages, and Cian got out a set of keys.

"Check out the view," he said and turned on his heel to face the way they'd come.

Max should have cracked some cheesy line while obviously looking at Cian, but—well, it was hard to flirt with his face on fire and his legs turning to rubber underneath him. His lungs were doing a fair job of trying to explode out of his chest too.

So instead, he simply turned to look at said view.

And—froze.

Below them lay the town, its dirt and dinginess drawn away by distance. It nestled in the bay, suddenly beautiful. And beyond it—

A great, glittering expanse. The shimmer of the rising moon off the Channel was hypnotic. This far out, the sea was still but for that waver of light over water. In the distance, the soft lights of a ship were sailing serenely across the darkness.

Max's breath caught in his chest.

"It's beautiful, isn't it?" Cian murmured.

It was more than beautiful. It was alluring. Coy. Dangerous—because from way up here, the sea looked so quiet and tame. So peaceful and powerless.

And she was anything but.

"I love the sea," Cian said and Max's gut clenched.

"Me too. My—my whole family's in the Navy."

"Really?"

"Yeah."

Cian laughed softly. "So's my stepdad. He's out there right now. Somewhere."

"You don't know where?"

"No. Mum worries more if she knows. So he doesn't say. We have to guess from his souvenirs when he comes home. What about yours?"

The peace and beauty was disturbed by the sharp pain in Max's throat.

He swallowed.

"Dead."

"Oh. Oh shit. I'm sorry, I—"

"I don't remember him," Max continued. "I was only three. But his whole family were in the Navy. All my uncles. Grandpa—"

His throat closed entirely.

Softly, Cian said, "Navy, too?"

"War," Max choked out, nodding.

"It's in your blood, then?"

He nodded again, rendered mute by the sudden wave of sheer loss as he stared out at the water. The water his father and grandfather had crossed a thousand times. The water he'd never be able to feel surging under a deck beneath his feet.

"Lucky," Cian said wistfully.

"What?"

"You. You're lucky. I've always wanted to go to sea."

"Really?"

"Mm. I could swim before I could walk. I love the water. But Mum never liked the idea of me going into the Navy. Not the place for people like me, you know? Took Dad two years of working on her just to get her to agree to letting me join the cadets."

Max's brain stalled.

"You're in cadets?"

"Yeah."

"Like—Sea Cadets?"

"Well, yeah."

Max finally tore his eyes from the shimmering sea and fixed them firmly on Cian. Imagining the uniform. The beret. Out on exercises, getting w—

His throat closed again for a wholly different reason.

"Why don't you join, if you like the sea and the Navy so much?" Cian asked.

"Cian."

"You could join up, no problem, we always have space. And the Navy like taking on ex-cadets. And—"

"*Cian.*"

"What?"

"Can we go inside now?" Max asked.

Because his throat was dry and his palms were sweaty. And his body suddenly cared nothing for the hill and Jazz's boots. It cared only about the boy in front of it, who had a cadet's uniform somewhere in his house and talked about the sea like other people talked about love affairs.

Max was interested.

Visibly so.

Cian's gaze flickered down and he briefly smirked.

Then slowly put the keys back in his pocket.

"No," he said softly and then bit his lip. Max wanted to pull it and kiss him, and he shifted his weight uncomfortably. "But..."

"But?" Max prompted.

Cian's gaze flicked down again.

Then he turned and began to walk along the little lane. Away from the cottages.

"Come on," he said. "There's a place where nobody will find us."

AT THE END of the lane was a gate.

Beyond the gate was a path through a wood.

And halfway along the path, just as the trees closed around them and swept them up in darkness, Cian's footsteps stopped and his hands were fists in Max's T-shirt, pushing. Guiding.

The bark hit Max's back, and then Cian's weight dragged.

Then they were sitting against a tree in the pitch black, and Max could hear Cian's breathing.

"Nobody ever comes down here?"

"Not at night," Cian whispered, and then his lips were on Max's.

Something about the darkness made it—sweeter. Sharper. *Seven for a secret, never to be told.* The old nursery rhyme whispered through Max's mind, and he felt his skin come alive in the silence. His fingers itched to touch. His body felt too tight. Cian was straddling one of his thighs, and Max wanted there to be no denim and cotton between their legs. Wanted skin. Just skin.

It was a lazy, hazy exploration though. Cian's hands stayed firm around the back of Max's head, catching him inescapable in that kiss. The gentlest grapple of them all.

But Max's hands had no such discipline. They wanted to touch, so they did. They smoothed over Cian's trousers, feeling the hard lines beneath. They cupped his hips, swiped at his stomach, and counted his ribs, rising and falling between them. They ghosted over his chest but learned their lesson from the sharp smack they were punished with, finding instead the long lines of his back.

And Cian felt—

Captivating. Incredible. Max could feel life—could feel passion, emotion, the crash and burn of every thought and every feeling under that invisible skin. He could feel Cian. Not the girl, not the boy, not the passage between the two. Just Cian. He wanted to feel that everywhere, all of the time.

He broke off to say it, but Cian's mouth simply found his neck instead. The teeth it put there were sharp and sensual, and Max could only breathe raggedly as things came undone—first his belt, then his jeans, then him. Cian's hands were sure and insistent, and Max could only gasp dumbly through it as the world changed beyond the darkness, as though time ran only outside the woods, and they were here, caught forever. As time slowly began to start again, Max found an overwhelming need to hold on. To grasp at that feeling—that simultaneous rush of power and powerlessness he'd felt in Cian's palm—and find it again. To capture it. To warm it, share it, and give it back.

And along with it, perhaps, undo Cian the way he could undo Max? Could he do that? Could he find places like that on Cian—unbottle the dangerous, devastating boy who had Max falling in l—

He caught at Cian's hand, damp and hot, at his belt.

"Let me—"

"No."

The voice was soft. The kiss that caught the corner of Max's mouth was even softer.

"Not yet."

Chapter Nineteen

MAX WAS GROUNDED for the whole weekend.

And he didn't damn well care. It was out of the way of people like Jazz and Tom. He couldn't grade with his face bashed to pieces anyway. And Cian—

God, Cian had put that buzzing under Max's skin, not just on his lips.

Max wasn't ashamed of his libido. He'd liked girls since he was thirteen. Boys since...six weeks ago, apparently. But he'd never actually done anything. Well, not with anyone. He was as acquainted with clearing his browser history and getting round the parental lock on his phone as any of the other boys at school.

But it turned out that whole 'you'll like it when you try it' thing was true. For him, anyway. He spent all weekend in his room with the door locked, remembering and reliving the feel of Cian's hand on his skin.

Who cared about being grounded?

It only got better when he was woken on Monday morning by an argument between Mum and Aunt Donna about whether he ought to go to school. For once, Mum won. So when Aunt Donna went out to work, Max got to stay at home and have a late breakfast with Mum, just like when he was little.

Only Mum wasn't upset like she'd been all the time back then. So, even better.

"You can help with some of the wedding plans," Mum said as she put his fry-up down in front of him. "And catch me up on this little thing with Cian, hm?"

Max paused, fork halfway to his mouth.

"Uh—"

"I take it that's where you went Friday night?"

"Um. Maybe?"

"And you had your date on Thursday…"

Max steadfastly refused to fill in the blanks.

"Do you have a boyfriend, Max?"

His chest caught at the B-word. It rolled over his skin, rubbing itself against his face like a happy cat.

"Yeah."

And his boyfriend liked to—do stuff.

Mum beamed and slid into the seat opposite, clutching her cup of coffee. "Tell me."

"Mu-um…"

"It is Cian, isn't it?"

"Yeah…"

"Mm, bet Donna didn't see that coming when she signed you up for boxing."

Max shrugged awkwardly, wanting to sink below the table. God, she had to know what they did Friday night. She had to. Why would she be asking if she didn't suspect?

"Can we not?" he blurted out. "It's just…you know. New."

"Everything starts somewhere," she said and propped her chin on her hand. "Are you going to be inviting him to the wedding?"

Max squirmed. "I don't know. Maybe."

"You should, you know."

"That's months away."

"Not very long now. You'll need to start coming to fittings soon. I've picked out a suit for you."

Max grimaced. He hated formalwear. It made him look even fatter than usual.

"Although with this boxing, I might have to change it for another."

Max paused, a spoonful of beans halfway to his mouth. "Why?"

Mum chuckled. "Oh, honey, look in the mirror. And check the size of your clothes lately."

Max glanced at the tumble dryer, in which his Friday jeans would still be waiting for their Monday evening turn on the ironing board.

"I thought you must've stretched them," he mumbled.

"Stretched what?"

"My jeans."

Mum rolled her eyes. "Denim doesn't stretch, sweetheart. You know when you came down to breakfast yesterday, you looked—"

Her voice creaked, and she stopped.

Max chewed on his lip and waited.

"You looked like your dad," she mumbled.

Max frowned.

"Really?"

He didn't know what his father had looked like, and the only picture Mum could bear to keep out on display was just a headshot. And he'd never really thought he looked like that picture. He looked like a Farrier, that was for sure—same fat build as Uncle John, same square jaw as Grandpa, even Grandma's thin, flat eyebrows. And he certainly didn't look anything like his pretty, skinny mum with her curls and dental-advert smile.

But his dad?

"Mm. Oh, go on. I suppose I can show you. Donna won't see."

She disappeared upstairs, and Max heard her rummaging around in her bedroom. He pushed his cooling breakfast away, oddly full despite only being half done, and peered down at himself. Mum had to be kidding. His gut was ballooning over his pyjama bottoms. His feet were white whales on the tiles. His breasts—well. Yes. Breasts.

Mum shuffled back into the kitchen and put a single photograph on the table.

Max stared.

The couple in it were immediately apparent. Mum hadn't changed in ever, and her bright laugh and windswept hair, captured forever in the photograph, were the same as if she'd put on an identical skimpy dress and gone down to the harbour right at that very minute to re-enact the image.

The harbour was different—still recognisably theirs, but simply different. Shops Max had never known. Little fishing boats that hadn't been sailed in years. A shiny new car parked just at the edge of the frame that hadn't been manufactured for eleven years.

And Dad.

Not a formal picture from a Navy record. But...

A towering monster of a man in swimming trunks and nothing else, with big ears and a bigger grin, an arm slung casually around his girlfriend's waist like he was some dumb jock kid with the entire world laid out before him. Like he was invincible. The kind of arrogant, happy, smug git everyone hated but nobody rationally knew why.

And he was massive. He towered over Max's mum, well over six and a half feet tall. He was even taller than Grandpa. Maybe even as tall as Uncle George, who had to duck to get through doorways.

He wasn't a beanpole like Grandpa, though—he was huge. Barn doors were smaller. His shoulders were wider than the doorframes Uncle George had to duck through, and his hips were so big Mum's arm couldn't get around them. He was obscenely large, an almost comical figure in the otherwise simple, standard little picture.

But—

He wasn't fat.

Max squinted at the man he didn't remember. He wasn't fat. He was enormous, probably the biggest man Max had ever seen, but...

Max could see the faintest traces of abs. His pecs were huge. His biceps bulged like a professional weightlifter's.

And there wasn't a trace of fat on him.

"He's—"

"Big?"

"Massive," Max said.

"I was only fourteen when we met, and he was just this fat kid down the street," Mum said softly. The word pinched at Max's ears and he frowned. "I loved him the minute he said hello. God, my parents were furious. He was eighteen years old, far too old for me, and just the son of those good-for-nothing Farriers. I was supposed to go to university, get a job in the city, be somebody. Not be mooning around after Fatso Farrier."

Max flinched.

"He was—"

"Yes, but—not like they call you. Nobody would have dared," Mum said, chuckling gently. "He was a monster of a man. Oh, very nice, such a gentle soul, just like you, but—well, I suppose people weren't so daring back then. And maybe having brothers helped. Certainly John could frighten the life out of you at thirty paces, so perhaps everyone thought messing with John Farrier's little brother wouldn't end well."

Max could imagine that. Uncle John's dullness did manifest itself as intimidating most of the time.

"It was just a nickname. All his friends called him that. And he would laugh about it. Even when—" She paused and swallowed and then began again. "Even when he drank, he was such a gentle man. The number of times the police would bring him home and say he'd been lovely all the way, they just didn't want him to fall into the harbour in the state he was in."

Max touched his fingers lightly to his father's smile. Fatso Farrier. Like father, like son.

But, like father, nothing like son.

"Do you still love him?" he whispered.

Mum's eyes shimmered and she coughed a wet laugh.

"Oh, God, yes."

Max bit his lip. "I'm sorry for what I said about him the other day."

"It's all right, darling."

"I shouldn't have said it."

"No, you shouldn't. But—sometimes I forget that you took your grandfather's death worse than his. You never really knew your father."

"Did he like me?"

She squeezed his wrist over the table.

"He adored you, sweetheart. I used to have to put you on the phone to him when you were just a tiny baby so he could hear you babbling. He never expected you—neither of us did—but he loved you from the very moment he found out you existed."

Max's mouth twisted in a smile. He knew that story. Mum hadn't told his dad at all. He'd come home from some deployment or other to find his fiancée with nine months of baby belly stuck out in front of her. They'd gotten married the following week, on a wet winter's morning at a registry office in Bude because it was the only one in the whole of Cornwall with an opening.

And he was born a week later.

"Would he—"

Max paused.

Swallowed.

"Would he have been..."

Mum squeezed his wrist a little harder.

"Been what, darling?"

"Disappointed."

She made a soft sound, and Max swallowed against an enormous lump in his throat.

"I'll never make the Navy," he mumbled hoarsely. "And I have a—a boyfriend. And I've been through so many schools because I'm a fat, usele—"

"Clever, kind, sensitive boy," Mum said softly.

Max sniffed. "Sensitive's not for the Navy."

"Oh, please. Your father used to write me poetry. Your soft streak didn't come from the Gardner side of your genes, sweetheart!"

Max laughed, a wobbly and feeble little sound.

"Honey. He would have been proud of you."

"W-why?"

"Because you are a Farrier, darling. That family took in a pregnant teenager because their son loved her. I mean, your grandma never even liked me, but she took me in anyway. That family looked after their son's widow and little boy when they could have washed their hands of the pair of us. Your Uncle John might be a boring old fart—"

Max spluttered a guilty laugh.

"—but he fought tooth and nail with the Navy to get your father classified as a death in service so they would pay us what was owed. And when I got together with Donna, where did your uncles go?"

"Nowhere," Max whispered.

"Nowhere. Exactly. We aren't their problem anymore, yet they're still family."

Max swallowed.

"You are just like them, Max. And your father loved every last inch of you then, and he still would now."

Max stared blindly at the photograph, his vision too blurred to see the captured smiles of his parents.

"You keep that," Mum said.

"'Kay."

"And if you want…"

Max scrubbed the tears away, took a deep breath, and prompted her to carry on.

"I—I know we haven't discussed it really, but…Donna wants me to take her last name when we get married."

"Oh."

"And I want to. I love her, and I want that."

"Um. Good?"

"But if you want to keep the Farrier name, then you do that."

He blinked.

It hadn't even crossed his mind. Mum would be Lucy Watts. And he'd be Max Watts.

Something deep inside recoiled. Some part of him, buried way down underneath everything, wriggled uncomfortably with the label.

It didn't fit.

"I don't want to be a Watts," he said, but…that didn't sound right either.

"Then don't."

"I mean…you know…it's not about Aunt Donna. I like Aunt Donna fine. It's just—"

"It's just, she's Aunt Donna."

Max opened his mouth…and then closed it. And nodded.

"I get it, sweetheart. It was too soon after your granddad died and…well. Honestly, I always thought you took Donna on far better than another boy might have done."

Max shrugged awkwardly.

"She won't be upset if you don't want to take her name, honey."

"It's not about her, though. If we were Gardners, maybe it'd be okay because Nana and Granddad suck—"

Mum laughed but didn't argue.

"—but we're not. And…it feels like leaving Grandpa behind."

And there it was.

It wasn't about his dad or his uncles. It was Grandpa.

It had always been Grandpa.

"Max."

Mum's hand stroked his wrist, and Max stared resolutely at the photograph.

"You're a Farrier. And neither of us—whatever we're called or wherever we go—will ever leave Grandpa behind."

Max turned his hand over to squeeze hers and felt that wriggly, unhappy place inside settle.

Chapter Twenty

CIAN WAS WAITING on the wall again when Max walked out of school on Tuesday.

"Hey," he said, grinning under a huge pair of sunglasses. "You like 'em?"

"You look like an aviator pilot."

"Is that a yes?"

"It's a no; you look like a poser."

"I look fantastic and you know it." Cian snorted and slid off the wall.

He did as well. Those combat trousers were back, and he had a blue T-shirt this time in a deep, rich shade that drew the eye.

"Oi, Fatso! That your girlfriend!" a voice yelled from the school gates.

Max's gut clenched, but Cian laughed and seized his tie, reeling in him for a sharp kiss.

"Let 'em stare," he whispered. "They're just jealous as fuck."

Max let his gaze wash up and down Cian's lithe form deliberately and raised his eyebrows.

"Um, duh?"

Cian grinned. "Oh, you're good for the ego. C'mon. Your place. I'm not digging that school uniform. I'll wait outside again."

Max let himself be towed. "Do you have to wait outside?"

"Yep."

"But...my room's more private than the woods," Max dared. "And I could close the curtains and turn the lights off if you want it to be dark."

Cian laughed.

"Oh no you don't. You and me on a bed, that will get regrettable."

Max squeezed Cian's hand.

"Why?" he asked eventually.

"Why what?"

"Why regrettable? Do you...I mean...Friday night was—"

"Best Friday night ever," Cian said, and Max's chest eased. "But I have zero self-control, and it was too mucky in the woods to be getting naked-naked, and your room has no such issues."

"And you don't want to get naked because...?"

"Because I'm not ready to yet," Cian said and pinched the inside of Max's wrist. "Keep that up and I'll change the plan."

"What is the plan?"

"Today? Nothing." Cian shrugged. "Just bum around and do stuff. I don't know. But when does your school break up for the summer?"

"Friday," Max said. "But I have exams for the two weeks after."

"So, that weekend, we're going swimming."

Max winced. "Um, I don't really swi—"

"Sea swimming. Not the leisure centre; that sucks."

Max shook his head doubtfully. "People—stare."

"There won't be people."

Max cocked his head.

"I can't exactly wear appropriate swimming clothes. You know what I mean?" Cian said as they passed into the park. "So I know a place you don't get other people very often."

Max's brain stalled and he coughed.

"Uh. So...by appropriate, you mean..."

"I mean, I should wear a bikini or a one-piece. But I can't. So I don't."

The mental image of Cian skinny-dipping on some lonely private beach was enough to shut down anything resembling thought, and Max made a strangled noise as Cian laughed.

"Nice to know that's what I can do to you."

"Excuse me," Max mumbled, "but were you there Friday night?"

"Ooh, true..."

They flirted—there was no other word for it but flirting—all the way home. And when Cian didn't let go of his hand and followed Max into the hall, Max's heart skipped several beats.

"Maybe I can come up for five minutes," Cian said, shrugging, and toed his shoes off.

"Maybe ten?"

"Don't push your luck."

Thankfully, Mum had a habit of invading and cleaning Max's room for him, so it wasn't a bombsite of crisp packets and biscuit crumbs. Cian flopped down in his desk chair, apparently very intent on no fooling around, so Max resigned himself to changing and finding something niceish to wear. The favourite jeans had been returned, but he had to rustle up another belt.

When he came back from getting his best T-shirt from the tumble dryer in the kitchen, Cian was holding his options form between finger and thumb.

"That's nothing," Max said quickly.

"Well, yeah, it's blank. What did you pick?"

"I—" Max coloured faintly. "I didn't. I'm going to go work in Aunt Donna's shop."

"A shop?" Cian said and frowned. "Oh. Sorry. I just thought you would be...doing something else. You know, you seem pretty clever, and you've got all these books..."

He ran his finger down the spines of the Aubrey-Maturin series stacked on Max's desk, and Max bit his lip.

"I like reading," he mumbled.

"They look heavy."

"They are. Kinda. But they're really cool too. It's all naval history and the secret service in the Napoleonic era, and—"

"And I barely manage a whole season of the same TV show," Cian said and laughed. "You're a dork. Why aren't you doing sixth form if you're such a dork? Does the shop pay good?"

"Well...no. It's...an apprenticeship really, and Aunt Donna's so..."

Cian frowned a little again. "Huh. So you're just...doing that?"

"I hate school," Max said. "I've been chased out of them constantly for being bullied."

"I still can't get my head round that," Cian said. "You have size twelve feet. I wouldn't have the balls to bully you."

Max glanced at the picture of his parents, now pinned to his corkboard.

At the behemoth that was his laughing father.

Fatso Farrier, Sr.

"Screw those idiots," Cian said and then hauled himself out of the chair. "C'mon. You want to go down to the harbour?"

"Sure," Max said.

The form fluttered back to the desk.

Blank.

THAT EVENING—LONG after Mum and Aunt Donna had gone to bed—Max got out of bed and sat down at the desk.

At the blank sheet of paper sitting where Cian had dropped it.

Max chewed on his lip.

What if—

He powered up the computer. Went to the Royal Navy website, so often perused for news and history and pictures of great hulking warships.

But this time, he clicked on the button he'd always avoided.

Recruitment.

Farriers weren't just Navy men. They were officers. Even Uncle George was an officer, and Max had it on good authority that Uncle George was charming, charismatic, and as dumb as a sack of soup.

So—

If Uncle George could do it…

Qualifications.

Max held his breath. Read the requirements. Counted points.

Only two.

He only needed two A-Levels to be over the threshold. One *B*, one *C* grade. Or an *A* and a *D*, even.

History would be easy. Mrs Pellow was always telling him so. He was good at history. And geography. And English, much as he hated Shakespeare. Or maybe he'd need something more maths and science-like? He was pretty good at chemistry. He got all *A*'s in his practice exams for chemistry…

He put pen to paper and paused.

Two more years.

Jazz. Aidan. Maybe Tom. Fatso Farrier, bumbling his way through two more years, wasting his time so the Navy could turn down a qualified loser instead of an unqualified one.

He swallowed.

Glanced up at the picture of his parents.

Glanced down at the paper.

Closed his eyes—and after a long minute ticked by, put the pen down.

And breathed out.

Chapter Twenty-One

"GOOD LUCK IN your exams, everyone, and I'm sure I'll see some of you next year."

Hubbub broke out in the classroom, but Max didn't move. Waiting until the last bag was slung over the last shoulder before standing up, he slowly made his way to the front.

"Mr Ryhill?"

His form tutor—and, more coincidentally, his religious studies teacher—glanced up from gathering his things.

"How can I help, Max?"

"I—I want to talk career options."

Mr Ryhill's look of complete surprise was like a punch in the gut.

"Really?"

Then the man seemed to gather himself and gestured for Max to pull up a chair.

"Well, I'm no Connexions counsellor, but I'll have a stab at it," he said. "What kind of thing do you have in mind?"

Max took a deep breath.

Then blurted his dream, for the very first time, into a space where it might actually matter.

"I want to join the Navy."

"I...see."

"I—I printed out their recruitment pages for officers. My dad was an officer. And his brothers were...were all officers, and my grandpa. And—"

Mr Ryhill took them, flipping through them easily.

"Hm, I see. These are quite generic, Max. Do you know what kind of role specifically you're after?"

"Maybe—maybe navigation. But I'm not sure yet."

"Well, from my limited understanding, the Navy is going to need people with skills in maths and science."

"Okay…"

"First step, I would say, is talking to a recruitment officer. Get a feel for what kind of roles there are, and then you can tailor your qualifications."

"My—my options form is late. Is it too late?"

Mr Ryhill's eyes softened.

"Officially, yes. Between you and me, I'm sure Mrs Pellow and I can rustle up an exemption for you."

"Really?"

"She's really very keen for you to go into history, you know."

"The Navy might not want history."

"No, but research and analytical skills will be a big bonus," Mr Ryhill said. "If I were you, Max, I would get some nice broad options for A-Levels. History will be an easy A for you, and that's a hundred points right off the bat. Then you only need another eighty for these general entry requirements. Now, I'm not sure your maths will be strong enough for the full A-Level, but maybe the AS?"

"Okay."

"Your chemistry grades have always been excellent—I know Mr Fraser is disappointed you didn't sign up for the A-Level—and perhaps PE?"

Max winced.

"I take it that's a no?"

"I hate PE."

"You'll have to pass the fitness requirement too, you know."

"Aunt Donna has me going to Muay Thai."

"Is that like kickboxing?"

"Kind of."

Mr Ryhill smiled again. "Well then, if you could demonstrate a commitment to sport, then that would certainly count in your favour. Tell you what. If you bring your options form to your exam on Monday, we'll make sure it gets processed. I'll give the recruitment office a call on Monday on my lunch break, and have a chat with them about any advice they can offer. You come and see me after your RE exam on Thursday, and we'll bash out a little plan, eh?"

Max fisted his doughy hands on his knees.

"D'you reckon I can do it, sir?"

Mr Ryhill scrutinised him.

"Honestly, Max? I would say no, for the way you're in the room but never here during my lessons," he said, very gently. "But Mrs Pellow—and Mr Fraser, for that matter—both consider you an excellent student. And Mr Fraser especially is not given to faint praise."

Max squirmed. Mr Fraser, the stony, humourless ghoul who taught chemistry, was not exactly Max's favourite.

"Given that? Yes, I do."

Max swallowed.

"Okay," he told his knees.

"Get the form in, Max. Do your best in your exams. Prove me wrong, and Mrs Pellow and Mr Fraser right, eh?"

Max cracked a faint smile.

"Thought teachers didn't like to be wrong."

"In this case, I would be glad to be wrong," Mr Ryhill said and then stood and gathered his things. "Go on, get out of here. You have to pass your GCSEs before you can jump at the A-Levels, you know."

Max shadowed him out of the building, not missing the sight of Jazz and Aidan loitering by the main gates, but Aunt Donna's van was idling on the side of the road, and his kit bag was on the passenger seat.

Screw Jazz and Aidan. He had a class to get to.

THEY ARRIVED EARLY. And Cian wasn't there yet.

Lewis was clearing up from his last class, whistling through his teeth as he stuffed pads back into a net, and Max automatically bowed at the edge of the mats in deference to Lewis's tutelage before approaching.

"Can I ask a favour?" he said before he could chicken out.

"You can ask," Lewis said with a dark chuckle.

"Don't tell Cian?"

"If this is something to do with him, I do not want to—"

"It's not, but...I just...don't want him to know yet."

Lewis eyed him warily.

"I—I'm looking into joining the Navy."

The wary side-eye didn't diminish.

"I talked to my form tutor today about which A-Levels to do, and he said I'd do well to do PE. But I hate PE, so—would you write me a reference for boxing? Like a record I can take to them when I need it?"

Slowly, Lewis put down the bag.

Folded his arms over his chest.

And grinned.

"Now where's that sulky little shit Donna brought to my classes, eh?"

Max reddened.

"I'll do you a deal, Farrier."

The use of his last name made Max jump.

"I will write you a reference if—and only if—you pass at least one grading in a class environment."

Max bit his lip.

"You do a grading class and pass it, the reference is yours. And it'll make 'em jump at the chance to have you. But only if you do that for me."

"Why?" Max asked honestly.

Lewis grinned.

"I told you, kid. There's a good boxer in there trying to get out. I think once you get your first armband and you feel that little weight round your bicep when you're trying to clobber Cian in the face again, it'll give you the boost you need."

The door banged. Cian's bag hit the wall and his top followed. Max eyed the mats, considering.

"We have a deal, Farrier?"

Lewis's hand hovered in the air, the wraps glowing white against his dark skin.

Max bunched his fat fingers into a fist.

One grading, which would form the baseline of all the others so was, by Cian's words, practically un-fail-able.

Just one. In class with all the other newbies. He could just get Cian to tell him when one with lots of newbies was coming up. Then he wouldn't be so embarrassingly out of shape.

And Lewis would write him a reference.

"Deal," he said.

His knuckles bumped Lewis's, and the instructor grinned.

"All right then," he said and raised his voice. "Thanks to Max's flash of ambition, today is going to be a fitness drill! Forget the gumshields, girlies, this is going to be a sweat day!"

Cian, loudly, called Max a soulless son of a bitch.

Chapter Twenty-Two

SOMETHING WAS SUPPOSED to happen Friday.

Max knew it, sure as he knew the sky was blue and Aunt Donna was psycho if her brother Damian was in town. Friday was the end of the summer term, the end of the school year—and the end of school always meant something happened.

Jazz and his bookends had traditions.

At the end of the winter term, they'd broken open Max's locker, put all of his things in the urinals, and pissed on them. At the end of the spring term, they'd put Max's head in the urinals, and pissed on him. This term—

It would be far worse than being pissed on, Max was certain. The last two terms, nobody had been expelled. Or even suspended. He'd denied he knew anything about who'd ruined his things at Christmas, and nobody even knew that Easter had happened at all.

This time—

He took precautions. Emptied his locker between first and second period, and carried his things from class to class. Texted his mum asking to be picked up at three thirty on the dot. Got out the bare minimum of things for his final lesson so he could escape as soon as possible.

But he was sweating his way through the film that was put on for them to watch. His armpits felt sticky. His fingers were trembling.

It wouldn't be enough. None of it would be enough.

The bell sounded like the downward swing of an executioner's axe.

He lurched up from his desk and was first out of the door.

The route to Mum's car was down two flights of stairs, along the main corridor, out of the double doors, across the courtyard between the humanities block and the science block, and out of the main gate.

The throng protected him. Everyone else wanted to do the same thing—get out, now, and start the summer.

But it would also betray him. Because Jazz and Aidan would be in the throng. And nobody would stop them. A crowd wouldn't prevent anything.

Max squared his shoulders and pushed.

And in carving his way through the gaggle of students, literally shouldering them aside, felling them like a tree crashing down through the undergrowth to the dirt below, Max realised Lewis had been right.

He was a big man. Big shoulders.

Not fat, but—big.

Fat didn't create this ripple effect of people moving round him. It wasn't dense enough. But he was shouldering his way through, and people were moving. Scowling and muttering, calling him an arsehole, but moving.

And there was Aunt Donna's van. Not Mum's car, but Aunt Donna's van, shuddering and stinking on the street. Idling. Waiting.

Safety.

"Oi, Fatso! What's your rush?"

The shout came from over his shoulder, and Max powered on. Sweat was starting to drip down his back. His thighs hurt. He was almost—almost—running. His lungs reeled as he shot past the gate—and then the door handle was cool in his hand and the cracked leather of the seat sticky and clinging to his uniform.

He slammed the door and shut out the school.

"Hello to you too," Aunt Donna said dryly, flicking on the indicator and peeling out into the mess of people and traffic. "Bad day?"

"No," Max said. They hadn't caught him. He'd escaped the end-of-term ritual for the first time ever. "Nothing happened. Just, you know. Summer holidays now."

"You say that now," Aunt Donna said. "Wait until you've been cooped up with your mum and her pre-wedding jitters for six weeks. You'll be begging to start early at the shop."

"Uh—"

She threw him a glance. "What?"

"I'm—maybe...not."

"Not what?"

"Shopping. I mean, apprenticeshopping. Shipping."

She cackled at his thick tongue.

"I mean," Max huffed, "that I talked to Mr Ryhill about putting in my options form."

"Oh?"

"And, um. He said it's late but...he'd try and sort it for me if I brought it in when I do my exam on Monday."

Aunt Donna said nothing at all for a long minute.

"I—I know it kind of—I should have said. Sorry."

"Sorry?" she muttered and then shook her head. "God, Max, you're a bright boy, but you're dense sometimes. I'm proud of you, you berk."

"Um—"

"Get your options form in, and to hell with the shop. What have you picked?"

"Not sure yet," Max mumbled.

"Well, history has to be one of them, right?"

"Yeah. Yeah, it is. But the N—"

He stopped himself, and Aunt Donna squinted at him as she flung the van round a turn.

"The what?"

"The Navy don't care about history," he mumbled, pressing his chin into his chest as though he could hide the words from her.

She breathed out.

"Oh."

"I just—I thought—I just had a crazy moment."

"Yeah," she agreed. "You had a crazy moment for years after your grandpa died that you'd let him down somehow and were a failure before you ever even tried. You had a crazy moment when you gave up on your Navy dream, when you turned your back on the sea and that salt water in your veins. And now maybe the crazy moment's over, huh? Maybe you're waking up at last?"

Max fidgeted, unsure of what to do with her—well, delight. Aunt Donna wasn't often thrilled with him like this.

"I can't do it," he mumbled.

"Of course you can," she said briskly. "I'll tell you what, Max. I'll do you a deal."

Max's knuckles tingled where they'd bumped Lewis's in the gym.

"If you do your A-Levels, I will take you on during the holidays as an apprentice anyway. We'll get you a decent certification—a nice practical skill to go with your book smarts and your boxing. And then it's just a case of acing the recruitment process, because with those three things on your applications, they'll want you."

A lump swelled in Max's throat. He blinked at the suddenly fuzzy windscreen and had to swallow to stop the burning sensation spreading into real tears.

"Deal," he croaked, and Aunt Donna reached over to briefly squeeze his shoulder.

"Tell you what," she murmured. "Just this once—just today—I'll let you skip the gym. How about it, eh? Want to pop into town and see if the model shop's got anything new in?"

Spend the evening sprawled out on the floor, piecing together that submarine he'd been eyeing up for a while? Instead of sweating, dying, and being shouted at by perpetually, annoyingly cheerful Lewis?

Max's thighs shifted, a sucking noise peeling them from the leather.

He shook his head.

"No. I made a deal with Lewis."

"Oh?"

"Yeah. He's—he's gonna give me a reference. For the Navy. If I grade."

Aunt Donna's fingers tightened on the wheel.

"So I gotta practice."

Finally, the white in her knuckles faded, and then she said, "I never met him, Max, but your grandpa'd be so proud of you right now."

It was the best thing Max had ever heard.

THE GYM WAS dead.

"All the schools are out, aren't they?" Cal boomed cheerfully from behind the desk. "Nobody wants to be boxing when they can be celebrating!"

Max smiled awkwardly, only half catching the sentence through Cal's thick accent, and lumbered towards the changing rooms. There were boys again, half a dozen maybe, talking about a football match. They ignored Max. He gratefully ignored them in return.

He'd brought a T-shirt this time. The tank top had somehow managed to give him a full-on nip slip the other day. And he had to tie the strings on his shorts. Staring down at himself in bewilderment, he wondered vaguely if Mum had stretched these in the wash too. There had to be something up with the machine.

But—

He turned his feet, examining them.

He could see—

Bone.

He could see his ankle bones. Only just, but there they were. Poking out of each side, shy and hesitant. There was a divide. Foot. Ankle. Calf.

"Jesus," he mumbled.

He stared in fascination at them as he padded out into the corridor and into the training room. He could see dense muscle under the flabby layer of waste.

"What's so amazing?"

Cian was doing the splits on the mats and stared at Max's feet too, although with a blank, uncomprehending expression. Max felt torn between showing off his feet and shamelessly staring at Cian's, um, position.

"I, uh. I lost my cankles."

"Your what?"

"My cankles."

Cian raised his eyebrows. "What the hell's a cankle?"

"You know, calf-and-ankle. When you can't see an ankle because your leg is too fat. I lost them."

"Uh—"

"I can see my ankles," Max clarified, sticking out a foot.

"Max, look down occasionally, yeah? You've had, uh, visible ankles for weeks."

"I have?" Max asked, still staring at his feet.

"Yeah."

"You sure?"

"Yes, I am very sure. I've been eyeing you up for a while now, and your feet have been in my ribs and stomach about three times per week, so..."

Max laughed. The sound—and the feeling—bubbled up in his chest like raw sunlight on the inside. And with it came this burst of...something.

He was going to put his options form in. He was going to get an apprenticeship anyway. He was going to get a reference from Lewis.

If—

If.

"Is there a class on?"

"Yeah. Mixed beginners."

"Can we go in there with them?"

Cian paused, dragged himself up out of the splits, and grinned.

"If there's room. How busy was the changing room?"

"Six or seven?"

"There's room. Come on then, big man. Let's show 'em what you got."

Chapter Twenty-Three

MAX HATED THE beginners' class.

But not for the reasons he'd feared.

Josh took beginners. Turned out Josh was a drill sergeant, or at least subscribed to a philosophy where if the students weren't grey with eyes rolling into the backs of their heads, they weren't training hard enough.

So it hurt.

And the others did laugh at him but not the way Max had imagined they would.

He'd imagined sniggers the minute he walked in, but nobody even frowned. A couple of girls with bodies like Olympic athletes had even nodded and smiled at him. He'd imagined disgust when he started to sweat all over the mats, but it turned out he wasn't the only one who sweated a lot. In fact, it turned out Cian was weirdly dry. Everyone was soaking. Towels went everywhere after the warm-up.

And when the laughter did start—

It was okay. Because it wasn't him. It was—well, no, it *was*, but it wasn't just him.

They had to line up and do head kicks on the training dummy. And Max hadn't done one before, so he not only missed, but overswung it and fell over. The ripple of laughter made his face burn. But then the girl after him did the exact same thing, and the same ripple swept through the room.

And Max...relaxed.

It wasn't nasty. It was just...kind of funny. It did look funny. The way the other foot slid made the tumble look almost deliberate and artificial. Like slapstick comedy. And when another guy managed to turn a head kick into a sort of strange roundhouse and managed to somehow bring the dummy down on top of himself, Max found himself chuckling along with everybody else. Josh rolled his eyes, called them all children, and the guilty party extracted himself from the rubber with a sheepish grin and a "Well, at least I didn't miss!" in his defence.

But for all the relaxation and that fear of sticking out a mile and being laughed out of class, Max did not enjoy the experience. He hobbled out, feeling like he'd been battered. He hurt way worse than the private sessions with Cian. And he felt disgusting. Worse, the changing rooms weren't empty. Somehow, he hadn't quite realised that particular side effect of going to a proper class.

And he needed a shower.

He couldn't not shower. He wanted to hang out with Cian after class. And Aunt Donna wasn't picking him up unless he called, so—

He sucked it up—and sucked in his gut at the same time— and stripped with shaking fingers.

All the confidence had been sapped out of him, along with a billion gallons of sweat. He kept his eyes on the floor as he shuffled towards the showers. They had no curtains, no cubicles. Just four showerheads jutting out of the wall, the water cascading down into a sunken tiled area in the floor.

He was two feet from another naked boy, and he could hardly breathe.

Fatso Farrier. Oozing into three times the space another kid would.

Roll up, roll up. See the fat freak in the flesh!

He scrubbed quickly, cringing with every shift of his folds, hunching in on himself in some pathetic attempt to look smaller. His chubby toes flexed on the tiles, and he stared resolutely at his ankles and tried to grasp at the glowing feeling they'd given him earlier. It could be worse. This could have been six weeks ago. Aunt Donna could have just signed him up for classes, not private classes. It could be worse.

But since when had 'it could be worse' made anyone even feel better?

He stayed under the cool spray until the last boy left the changing rooms and then fumbled into a towel and back into his clothes with a burning embarrassment in his face. Covering up the fat with fabric helped Max pull himself together, and he sat in his jeans and T-shirt, staring at his bare feet for another long minute.

And then someone knocked on the door.

"Uh—"

"Max?"

Cian. Max relaxed. "Yeah. Sorry. Just coming."

"You alone in there?"

"Um, yeah—"

The door cracked open, and Cian slipped inside. His hair was sticking up, darker with water, and he'd changed into some jeans tight enough he must have been poured into them. And, uh. Tight enough to show off...something else too.

Max reddened, and Cian followed his gaze before smirking.

"Always pack in tight clothes," he said. "Helps people remember what I am."

"Uh—unfairly attractive?" Max tried.

"Smooth," Cian said. "You about ready to go?"

"Uh, yeah, yeah, s—"

The word was cut off with a squeak as Cian sat down in his lap.

On it. Facing Max.

Straddling him.

And with Cian's surprisingly heavy weight straddling his lap, and both of Cian's pale hands braced on the wall by Max's head, and Cian's tongue in Max's mouth, Max's body sort of...stopped listening to his brain.

It seemed only polite to steady Cian. Make sure he didn't fall off or anything. And if a hand on his arse was a good way of doing that then...well. Manners. It was just being polite.

And given they were dating, and Cian really was unfairly attractive, it would be quite rude of Max not to reciprocate to Cian kissing him like—well, like that.

Air.

On his ear. Whispering.

"The look on your face when you got that head kick right was hot as fuck." And then Cian's hands weren't on the wall anymore. "So call this positive reinforcement."

"Um," Max squeaked. "Are you—are you going to do this every time I get a new move right?"

"Maybe," Cian breathed, and Max shivered as he felt Cian's tongue on his ear. "You got a problem with that?"

"Nope. No. Absolutely not. No problem. It's all good. It's goo—*oh*."

Just coming, indeed.

"ONE DAY," MAX said when they reached the bottom of the stairs outside, "you're going to let me touch too, right?"

Cian winced.

"I mean, you know, I don't have to, like, whatever you're okay with. But it just feels kind of weird that you do that to me, but I've not—" Max was interrupted with a short, sharp kiss.

"Shut it."

Max shut it.

"At the risk of sounding like a romance novel—it's not you, it's me."

"You—don't want me to?"

A little shard of hurt buried itself in Max's chest. It wasn't exactly surprising—who would want Max's fat hands all over them—but Cian didn't seem to mind otherwise? If he didn't want Max to touch him, why would he want to do what he'd just done upstairs?

Cian blew upwards into his hair.

"It really isn't you. I want to and I don't at the same time. And it's nothing to do with it being you. It's—me."

Max blinked.

Then caught on. Ish. "Is this to do with your, um..." He fished for a word and eventually offered, "Layout?"

"My layout?"

"Yeah. Your, uh. Design."

Cian snorted and then began to snigger behind his hand.

"Well, I don't know the terms," Max whined, and Cian shook his head.

"No, sorry. That's just—brilliant. Never heard that one before. My layout. I like that. And—yeah. It kind of is that."

Max fidgeted. "Well. Um."

He didn't really know what to say. Somehow, he felt that pointing out he liked girls too would earn him the mother of all cold looks, and possibly a punch in the face.

"You did something brave today."

What?

"Uh. Thanks?"

"Going to a class. You really didn't want to go last we spoke. And I saw your face when you went to get changed. You hate changing rooms."

Max shrugged awkwardly. "Yeah, well..."

"Don't argue."

"Okay."

"Say, 'yes, Cian, I did something brave today.'"

Max rolled his eyes. "Fine. Yes, Cian. I did something brave today."

"Good."

Cian rocked forward on his toes. This kiss was everything the earlier kisses weren't. Soft. Chaste. A breath of sensation against Max's lips. A hum, gentle and reverent, rather than the electric buzz of excitement.

Max's heart expanded like a balloon in his chest, huge and overwhelming.

"Tomorrow, I'll do something brave for you."

Max swallowed.

"Don't care," he mumbled and closed the gap again.

He didn't care about anything but this.

Chapter Twenty-Four

"MUM, CAN YOU give me a lift to Cian's?"

It was half seven in the morning. Max had been given instructions. Which were unfair, delivered mid-kiss as they had been, but Max was getting the impression that Cian wasn't very fair sometimes.

"What," Mum said. "Right now?"

She was in her dressing gown, eating toast and flicking through a bridal magazine.

"Um. Please?"

She sighed but finished her toast and brushed the crumbs off her hands. "All right, but I'm not getting out of the car."

It was brilliantly sunny already, the car uncomfortably hot, and Max wound the window down and rested his arm on the gap. He had a bag with his swimming trunks, towel, and a change of clothes, but he wasn't sure what Cian really had in mind. Swimming in the bay was dirty, and there was no way Max was going to be laughed at in the leisure centre.

"Might be back late," he said anyway, and Mum shrugged.

"Got your phone?"

"Yeah."

"Emergency money?"

"Tenner in change."

"Okay then. Back by ten."

"Eleven?"

"Ten."

He didn't push further (she usually said eight, like he was a kid) and instead watched the town roll by out of the window. It was dry and dusty. It hadn't rained in weeks. Max could only hope that if Cian's exhibitionist streak got some air today, it would choose a shady spot.

The cottages at the top of the hill were crowded by dying flowers, wilting in the heat. The front door to one of them was open, a ten-year-old Land Rover idling by its gate. At the sound of Mum's tyres crunching on the dirt track, Mrs Williams came out of the open door, shielding her eyes against the sun. She looked even bigger than that day in the gym, wearing a sleeveless top and black leggings, and her beaming smile was blinding.

"Cian! It's Max!"

Max smiled awkwardly back as he fumbled his way out of the car.

"Ten!" Mum repeated loudly, and he huffed.

"Okay, okay. Ten." He patted his pocket to show her the outline of the phone and closed the door.

"May as well hop straight in the car, sweetie," Mrs Williams said. "Cian's asked me to drop you both off on my way to Katie's horse-riding lesson."

Cian chose that moment to emerge, in one of those clingy T-shirts and the favoured combats, and herding a little girl ahead of him. Katie, it turned out, was Cian's six-year-old half sister. She looked cute, with a frizzy bun and huge dark eyes, but she was deafening, screeching in delight as they drove down the hill.

"Um, don't you have to drive this way every day?" Max asked Cian.

"Yep," came the bored reply.

"And she does this every time?"

"Yep."

"And you still have hearing in both ears?"

"Dumb luck."

Cian's mum laughingly chided him for being mean, and Max decided to hell with being polite and put both hands over his ears as Katie squealed at going round a roundabout. Mrs Williams wasn't even speeding. God, the kid ought to drive with Aunt Donna.

Cian said nothing of his plans as they left the town behind and headed into the baking countryside. Swifts soared above the car, little black dots in an endless blue. Crickets were humming loud enough that they punctured the sound of the engine and Katie's yelling. A kestrel, perched on a lonely fencepost, regarded them with cold calculation as they swept by.

And beyond Cian, beyond the tinted glass of his window, Max could see the sea.

Mrs Williams pulled over at a seemingly random point in the dusty road and told Cian that if he didn't call to be picked up by four, she'd leave him for the fishes.

"Sure, Mum. Thanks, though."

And then—

They were alone.

In a vast, flat plain of dry grass and barbed wire fences, with the sea an endless blue strip on the horizon.

"So what are we doing here?" Max asked.

Cian laughed and held out his hand.

"Swimming."

"In grass?" Max asked doubtfully.

"Uh, no, nobody needs grass blades in sensitive places." Cian pointed at the sea. "In that, you moron. Now c'mon, don't leave me hanging."

Max took his hand and, once again, trusted Cian.

And it paid off.

The fields ended abruptly in a cliff. Below it lay a bay, tiny and nestled into the coastline like it had been punched in— an almost complete circle bitten out of the landscape. The path was not as treacherous as it looked, but was narrow and uneven, and they had to go single file. The sun beat down on the rocks as they scrambled downwards, but Max felt an old thrill, a half-forgotten pleasure in the dust coating his fingers from the climb.

How long had it been since cliffs and coastlines? He must have been a kid still. Bouncing down them with Uncle George while Grandpa grumpily insisted he was too old for such nonsense and would go and wait at the ice-cream parlour.

That hadn't been here; that had been near Land's End, ten years ago now. But the dry rock felt the same, and the gentle rush and swell of the sea, the salt in the air, the breeze tugging at his hair in friendly swipes, was all as it had been then.

The moment Max's feet hit the beach, he toed his shoes off.

It was rocky—made of a thousand shades of blue, grey, and white—and a bright blue sea, shallow and serene, lapped at its edge. The cove was sheltered; beyond it, Max could see the white foamy tops of proper waves.

"It's so quiet."

"Nobody comes here."

"Why?"

"All the other coves down here are sandy. This one's not."

"Why?"

"Dad says the cliff collapsed and the sea's not had time to wash it all away yet. Too sheltered."

Max could believe that. The cliffs were sheer but suspiciously bereft of weeds, tiny trees, and birds' nests. A couple of huge boulders jutted crudely from the beach. Rock pools littered the surface, murky and—he was sure—teeming with life.

"It's so still."

"The next one up—towards Falmouth—is where all the surfers go. And the next one back towards Plymouth is where all the families go. This one? Nobody. During the day, you get bonfires and campers up in the fields at night sometimes."

Max stared out at the sea and felt the pull.

He wanted to swim. Wanted to feel the salt on his skin. Wanted to be cool and hot at all once. The slide of sand between his toes, invisible. The weightlessness. To bob along the surface, powerless and trusting.

To let the sea take control.

He dropped his bag and his jeans.

With only Cian for company, the shame of the changing room was a distant memory. Max simply stripped. And when he was naked as the day he was born and opened his bag to find his trunks, Cian's soft laugh disturbed his focus.

"Don't."

"Don't?"

"Go naked," Cian said and a grin widened across that freckled face.

Max paused.

"It's just you and me." Cian licked his lower lip. His gaze dropped—as did Max's blood. "Trunks might get in the way later."

Whatever blood remained in Max's face left it, and he coughed.

"Well. Uh. Swim naked. Okay."

Cian's laugh followed him down to the water. But only when Max had waded far enough that the water reached his shoulders—thereby hiding his overkeen response to Cian's words—did he stop walking and turn around.

"Is it cold?" Cian yelled from the shoreline.

"Not bad!"

It was cold, but the heat of the sun on his head and neck was a pleasant counterpoint. Max experimentally swam a couple of strokes further into shore and decided to sit on the shallow rock and sand seabed to wait for Cian.

Who seemed to hesitate.

For what seemed like an age (though really it was probably only five minutes or so) Cian hovered on the shoreline. He'd changed his shorts for swimming trunks, but seemed to dither about his T-shirt. Eventually, he turned his back to Max and the water and removed the shirt and the vest underneath. And, to Max's surprise, put the T-shirt back on.

Then Cian turned and waded into the water with a speed that spoke of sheer determination.

"You're going to swim with your shirt on?" Max called.

"Not all of us tan, Max!"

Somehow, Max felt that wasn't quite why, but he left it. Cian sprawled out in the water like a starfish and then turned on his front and walked on his hands to Max, dragging his floating body along behind like a boat. Max grinned at the sight and mimicked it until a gentle wave rushed them both and they had to swim for real.

"And it is cold," Cian complained, but he was grinning.

The T-shirt was forgotten, as was Max's lack of clothes. Max hadn't gone sea swimming in an age, and Cian was a self-confessed water baby. They...played. Like kids. Cian was mean with splashing, and Max's retaliation of dunking didn't seem to do anything to stop it. And in the cool water, rushing and swelling gently around them, Max felt—

Home.

He felt at home. Good. Happy. Relaxed. And it felt like the first time since Grandpa had died. The salt was clinging to his face, tingling and pleasant. The power of the ocean between his fingers and toes. The edge of warning even as the sea toyed with them peaceably enough. It could turn. It tolerated their presence, appreciated their happiness, but nothing more. It wasn't there for them.

But the sea took more energy than the pool, and eventually Max tired. He dragged himself to some rocks below the cliffs, enjoying the refreshing spray of waves breaking softly over his stomach as he propped himself up and stretched out his legs to float, white and wobbly under the waves.

"Tired?" Cian called, starfishing in the swell.

"Yeah."

"Could always sunbathe. Get an all-over tan."

"Too hot," Max complained.

Cian rolled over in the water and struck out for him. His hands were cool and alien under the water when they gripped Max's ankles and peeled his legs apart, and then he was resting his chin on Max's chest, far too close and far too tempting, and grinning.

"You," Max said seriously, "would in no way help cool me down."

"No," Cian agreed.

"Unless you were on Mars."

"Even then, I'd just send you dick pics."

"From Mars?"

"Nothing else to do."

Max laughed. Cian grinned, drifting away again, and then he surged back and scrambled up on the rocks. He came completely clear of the waves, water streaming from his clothes, and Max—

Stared.

The trunks were a solid dark green, and though they clung, they gave very little away. But the T-shirt was white, rendered see-through from its soaking. And suddenly there was shape where he'd never seen shape before.

Cian shifted a little and hunched his shoulders.

"Um. Sorry. Sorry."

Max tore his gaze away towards the open ocean and tried to breathe. But—he'd seen them. The dark shadows of...well. The soft swell of—um. Shape. And. They were—nice.

Really nice.

And Max was human. And humans sort of...stared at stuff. And wanted to touch stuff. Especially the nice stuff, with dark shadows and shape.

He gulped for another breath and sank a little deeper into the water. That would help. Or at least hide it.

"You were brave yesterday," Cian said softly above him, "and I'm going to be brave today."

"You don't have to," Max said.

"If I can't be brave with you, I might never be."

Max wasn't sure what being brave even was, for Cian. He'd told a total stranger in a boxing gym what he was. He'd made a lesbian joke to another stranger in a bus stop. That was, like, the bravest thing ever.

"Come up here."

"Um. I might need a minute first."

Cian chuckled. "I don't mind if you don't."

"Um. Okay. Just—sorry."

Max hauled himself up to sit beside Cian without looking, his movements a little stiff and awkward thanks to his predicament—and the moment he did, Cian slid down into the water, the darkness swallowing him whole. He bobbed back up, shaking water from his now dark-blond hair.

"Okay," he said, as if to himself. "I can do this."

Max said nothing.

Then Cian performed some sort of—wriggle.

And threw his trunks up onto the rocks.

Max's brain stalled. "Uh," he said. Uh, indeed. Cian had entered the water wearing trunks and a T-shirt. Now the trunks were on the rock. And Cian was in the water. So. Yeah. Mathematically speaking—

Cian ducked under the water entirely. For a moment, all Max saw was a pale, indistinct motion under the gentle rocking of water around the rocks.

And then, sopping wet white slapped the rock, and the maths equation was completed.

Cian plus T-shirt plus trunks had entered the water.

Now the water held Cian, and the rock held the T-shirt and the trunks.

Ergo.

Yeah.

Cian surfaced—a little. Only his head and neck cleared the water, but it was hardly a filthy river, and Max could see the hazy, water-distorted skin below.

"Uh," he said.

Cian kicked out and drifted a little farther away. Another kick.

And Max slid down into the water.

Silently, he struck out, and they came back together in the middle, away from the rocks and the shore, just two souls drifting in an infinite sea. And Max wanted to—

What? Touch? Talk? Examine and explore, or enthuse and excite?

Cian's arms looped around his neck. Cian's mouth was wet on his own, marked with salt and sweetness. He tasted of the sea.

And under the water, Max could feel—

Feel.

Instinct wanted to touch the shadow and shape he'd seen through the wet T-shirt. But something else—something smarter, something Max hadn't even realised was there— whispered that maybe it wasn't the time for his instincts. Later. But not right now.

So he deferred to the second one. To the one that had struck him in the gym, what seemed like a thousand years ago, when Cian had so shamelessly turned his back and stripped.

He stroked both hands down an uninterrupted back, a column of skin and spine, soft and smooth.

Pulled.

They fit together like puzzle pieces, tight and sure.

Between them, Max could feel—everything.

But it was against his lips, around his neck, in the grip on his shoulders, in the way the chest against his own hitched when his hands settled in the small of that unblemished back, that Max could feel Cian.

Chapter Twenty-Five

"Cian?"

"Mm?"

"You're burning."

Cian didn't move but for the faint quirk of his lips into a smile.

The sun was dipping towards the horizon, but its heat had dried their naked bodies on the shore, collapsed mere feet from the sea like landed fish. Maybe whales. The tide was creeping inwards in tiny inches, the surf kissing their feet now. Max hauled himself onto his back and sat up to watch the water stroke at Cian's calves.

His eyes, completely dismissive of his brain's demand not to stare, drifted higher.

Cian was the picture of serenity now—arms tucked under himself, freckled back and endless legs (and everything between) exposed to the sun, fair hair burned almost white and stiff with salt—but there had been something in the death grip on Max's neck that had been nothing to do with trying to kiss and tread water at the same time.

Max knew he ought not to stare at the naked body Cian had been careful not to show him.

But—

He tore his gaze away again and picked up a pebble. Flung it. It punched through the water with a satisfying plunk.

"What you doin'?" Cian mumbled, not opening his eyes.

Max's gaze flickered down to Cian's elbow, relaxed by his side, and the gentle swell he could just about glimpse between rib and rock beyond.

He glanced away guiltily.

"Sorry," he said on autopilot, and then a prickle of awareness trickled up his spine.

Even without looking, he knew Cian was watching him.

"For what?"

Max's brain wanted to ask questions. Max's body wanted to extend a foot and nudge Cian over onto his back and get another look. Or a first look. Apart from that glimpse of shape and shadow through the T-shirt, Max hadn't seen a thing. And there was something scary and dangerous skirting around the edges when it came to that sort of thing. Something he didn't understand.

"Staring," he said eventually.

Cian let out a long breath. His arm moved. Out of the corner of his eye, Max saw those long, pale fingers begin to toy with a couple of pebbles.

Silence.

Then, so quiet Max barely heard it, Cian said, "You looked at me like you wanted to bite me through my T-shirt."

The thought had occurred.

"Uh—"

"You touched me like you wanted to get right inside me and find out all my secrets."

That thought had occurred too.

"And you're always staring."

Max swallowed. His tongue felt thick and clumsy in his mouth.

"Close your eyes."

"What?"

"Your eyes. Close them."

Max obediently closed his eyes.

"Keep them closed."

"Okay."

"If you peek, I'll drown you."

Max wasn't entirely sure that was a threat rather than a promise, so he scrunched up his face, demonstrating they were properly closed and all.

Then—

"Oh."

Skin. Weight. Warm and heavy. Smooth but for the faintest catches of salt.

He knew this position. It had been a changing room then, and there'd been clothes. But now—

Cian's thighs were bracketing his hips. Those shadow-shapes were touching Max's chest. A hand was kneading Max's stomach lightly, like a cat flexing its claws. Warning.

And there were lips against his own.

Max's fingers twitched—as did something else. Was he allowed to touch? Please say he was allowed to touch.

"Cian," he breathed. "This is a really, really dumb idea."

"Why?"

Max whimpered when the question was kissed into his jaw, and he felt the faintest touch of teeth.

"I'll—you know. I'm—"

Cian's weight shifted back slightly and brushed the problem. Max groaned.

"I know."

Max balled his hands into fists by his sides and clenched his jaw. Eyes closed. Eyes closed.

"This," he mumbled decidedly, "is cruel and inhumane."

Cian laughed.

"What?"

"This is against my human rights."

"Get you, lawyer-boy. Screw the Navy, you ought to be in Parliament."

The flash of levity helped—kind of. Because when Max laughed, Cian's weight shifted, and then his brain short-circuited. All he could feel was skin and soft hair and want, Jesus, so much want.

"I stare because I want you all the time," Max blurted out into the self-inflicted dark. "And you don't really like it, so I'm sorry, and I'm trying not to, but it's hard."

"It's definitely hard."

"Shut up," Max whined.

Cian kissed him. But it was soft and tentative, nothing like the flash of humour and flirtation.

"I'm all scrunched up inside, Max," he whispered there.

"What?"

"In my head. I want things. I like things. But then I hate myself for wanting them. Hate the way I like them. Does that make sense?"

No. "Um…"

"Give me your hand."

Max raised it uncertainly. Cian smoothed it out, spreading the fingers flat—and then Max shivered when his palm was pressed to something unmistakeable.

"Um—"

"You like that?"

Max fought not to squeeze. Oh God. Holy hell, he was touching Cian's—

"Y-yes."

"Me too."

Max sensed a but. Sweat was breaking out in the small of his back. His libido was on an ecstatic loop, but he ruthlessly crushed it. Not. The. Time.

"But it makes me feel like something I'm not, too. Makes me feel like—I'm not real. I'm not right."

Max tugged his hand away and closed it into a fist around the air.

"It didn't feel like that in the water."

Wait.

What?

Cian's lips hovered close. Max could feel his breath.

"Come back in the water with me?"

Max licked his lips, nearly catching Cian's.

"To do what?"

"Maybe you could get right inside of me and find out all my secrets?"

Max whimpered.

"Oh God."

Cian's smile against his skin was as clear as if Max had seen it.

"Let's play hide and seek. You count to ten. I'll go hide. Then you come and find me. Deal?"

"Deal," Max said quickly, his heart pounding somewhere way lower than his chest. "One. Two—"

The weight on his hips disappeared. Pebbles crunched. Feet splashed clumsily through water, and Max felt a momentary coolness at being left behind.

He counted. Opened his eyes. Staggered to his feet and crashed into the water.

The pull to the sea had never been so strong.

"OH DEAR LORD," was the first thing Mrs Williams said. "Aloe vera for you."

Cian rolled his eyes, but Max had to privately agree. He was going to look like a red lava lamp by the morning.

"Did you have fun?" she asked as they clambered in the back seat, dumping their wet bags in the footwell.

"Yeah. Swam. Sunbathed. Had to defend lunch from seagulls. The usual. Right, Max?"

"Uh-huh."

Cian smirked at him and turned away to stare out of the window. He kept shifting in his seat, maybe uncomfortably and...maybe Max couldn't entirely blame him.

Okay. Fake nothing was up. Max could do that. He copied, peering out of his own window, but he felt laughably obvious. His skin felt too small, and he was pretty sure it wasn't the dried salt crackling along the hairs of his arms.

It felt rather like he'd left his ability to breathe in the ocean.

And maybe his ability to stop grinning.

But who the hell cared how stupid he looked, beaming out of the open window at swallows diving over the fields and the streaks of silvery blue as the very first hints of dusk splayed out across the sky?

His phone beeped, and he fumbled for it. It would be Mum. Should he go home? He should go home. But—he stole a glance at Cian out of the corner of his eye—he wanted to not, too. But then there'd be no, uh, bodies of water at Cian's house. Not big enough for two, anyway. So he should go home. He didn't want to make Cian—

I'm so uncomfortable right now.

Max blinked at the text and then side-eyed the sender.

Who was serenely ignoring him, staring out of the window like he was lost in his own head.

Why? Max replied.

Water.

What about water?

It's inside me, that's what!

Max choked back a laugh.

Salt water is not okay inside.

I'll take your word for it.

Next time we find a hot tub.

Max rolled his eyes. *Uh good luck with that.*

Thanks :)

Max blinked, the humour dissolving.

For what?

Listening.

You didn't say anything.

Yeah, but you listened. So I didn't have to.

Chapter Twenty-Six

FRENCH.

Sweat was running down Max's back in thick, disgusting streams. It was obscenely hot in the corridor, and the dull drone of Mr Ryhill's voice was like a bluebottle kissing a microphone. Annoying, repetitive, and just grating enough to keep Max on edge.

Chemistry.

He'd come straight from his exam. Just like Mr Ryhill had said. Only now, sitting and sweltering in the corridor, Max had to ask himself why he was bothering. He only had a few more weeks to go at the gym. Then he'd have a guaranteed apprenticeship with Aunt Donna. Followed by a steady job. So it wasn't glamorous, so what? Somebody had to sell screwdrivers.

Maths.

But that euphoric feeling from the beach had still been with him when he'd got up to go to his exam that morning, and Max had shoved the options form into his bag without thinking. Now he was clutching it in one clammy hand and wondering why the hell he was even thinking about two more years at this place.

History.

Mrs Pellow. Cian. Lewis. Aunt Donna. Mr Ryhill.

It was all their fault, Max tried. But that didn't stick. It wasn't theirs. He was his. He ought to have learned his lesson about dreams by now.

The bell rang. He jumped, the paper shivering in his hand. Chairs scraped in the classroom behind him. Mr Ryhill's voice rose.

And then the corridor was filling with students, and Max's body was on autopilot. Standing.

"Ah, Max, come in."

Max stuck out his arm, holding the form out like it was a bomb in front of him.

"Is that it?"

"Yes."

"Well, take a seat. Let's have a look."

Mr Ryhill plucked the paper from Max's hand like it didn't matter, and Max wanted to snatch it back and tear it up. He had to be crazy. Two more years of this? He'd only fail. He failed at everything else; what made him think that he could do A-Levels? What made him think they'd change anything?

"Now, I had a word with someone at the recruitment office in town," Mr Ryhill was saying, and Max fought to tune in, "and they emphasised practical skills and fitness above academia, unless you have a specialist degree such as mechanical engineering. Are you thinking of university, Max?"

"What? No!"

"You should."

Max was brought up short.

"I talked to Mrs Pellow after you came to see me last week," Mr Ryhill continued, blithely flipping through his folder and not looking at Max whatsoever, "and she's convinced you have the aptitude for an excellent history degree."

"History—history won't get me into the Navy."

"No, but the Officer Training Corps would."

"The—what? That's the army."

"And many of their students go into the RAF and the Navy as well," Mr Ryhill said, finally looking up. He peered over his glasses at Max and smiled. "It's practical training—paid as well, so it helps with the cost of a degree—and it's an excellent fast-track route. You should seriously think about it."

"Um. Maybe just think about the A-Levels first," Max mumbled.

"All right. Mrs Pellow has said she'll make room in her classes if there isn't any, so that will be fine. There's always space in maths, though Mr Gregory warns it's a big jump from the GCSE, so you might struggle. He suggests getting hold of the textbooks over the summer and putting in some early practice."

Yeah, like Max was going to do that.

"I don't think French is going to work in here though," Mr Ryhill said, tapping the form. "It runs alongside most of the sciences, so that's going to clash, I think. Have you another option in case you can't take French?"

"Um. I don't know."

"Well, is there another subject that interests you?"

"I dunno," Max mumbled, feeling his face flush. "I'm good at geography, I guess."

"Well, we'll put that as a secondary option if French doesn't work out, eh?"

Max shrugged awkwardly. None of it was going to work out. He was crazy for even thinking—

"And Mr Fraser wants to see you."

"What?"

Oh no. No-no-no-no. Not Freaky Fraser. He was the creepiest teacher in the entire school. He looked like Gru and was about as friendly as Lurch. What the hell did he want to talk to Max for?

"Why?"

"I couldn't say, Max. He wants you to pop along to his classroom after you're done here—S4."

"I—I have to—"

Mr Ryhill pinned him with a stern look, and Max shrank back in his seat.

"I'm pleased you're finally showing some initiative about your future, Max," he said, "but it has to last. Don't mess us about, now."

"I'm not—"

"I know you've had issues at school—"

Max wanted to ask what the school—any of the schools—had ever done about it.

"—and it's affected your academic performance, but you have to recognise that we're giving you a chance here. Normally, I would say if your form wasn't in on time, tough luck. We're making an exception for you, and it's going to take a lot of work to get you into these classes. Some of the teachers have already made up their lists and won't hear of new additions, you know."

Part of Max wanted to demand they put that effort into getting Jazz and his stupid mates off his back, instead of making sure he could take freaking A-Levels to be a qualified failure. But the other part—the part that shrank back from boys shorter than him with sneers wider than his streak of cowardice—wilted.

"Sorry, sir," he mumbled instead.

"Now, these are all contingent on your exam results just like everyone else. If you pass them all highly enough, then the only question mark I would have is French. But if not, geography. All right?"

"Yes, sir."

Mr Ryhill handed over a pale grey photocopy of the form and smiled. It didn't reach his eyes.

"Now go and see Mr Fraser before you head off home."

Max let himself out of the classroom with a sick feeling in his gut, two parts misery and one part anger. Who was Mr Ryhill to have a go at him anyway? Nobody ever kicked Mr Ryhill in the head at school. Nobody threatened Mr Ryhill's boyfriend just for being associated with him. Nobody ever—

"Oi! Fatso!"

Shit.

The shout arose the moment he'd stepped into the courtyard between the humanities block and the science block, and he ducked his head and hurried forward. The cool shadows of the science corridor washed over him as he rushed inside—but the school was quiet, the next exam having begun and all the other classes in progress, and the bang echoed behind him.

The hand that seized his belt was hard. The slam of the toilet door on his head was harder. And then he was on his knees on the cracked tiles, dizzy with the speed of it all, and a pair of boots were in his eyeline.

Timberlands.

His gut seized up.

"Kiss 'em then, Fatso."

Max pushed himself back on his hands and shakily stumbled to his feet. Tom was leaning against one of the sinks. Arms folded. Scowling.

And when he turned to go, Jazz was against the door—with Max's options form in his hand.

"What's this, Fatso?"

"My—my options form."

"Your options are a stroke or a heart attack. This shit says French. You gonna learn to speak French, Fatso?"

"It's for A-Levels."

"I know what it is, you fucking retard!" Jazz exploded.

Max flinched back, and then a savage blow to the back of his legs brought him to his knees again. The bone cracked painfully on the tile.

"I don't think that's fair," Jazz said, his voice suddenly even again. "You got Tom expelled, and now you're trying to stick around another couple of years. You've got some nerve."

Max shivered. His gut hurt. His knees were fat slabs of blubber on the floor. When the next blow came—a blur of tan and a heavy thump into his kidneys—he was catapulted forward.

Then a weight pressed down on his back.

A boot.

"Apologise."

"M'sorry, Tom—"

"Better than that."

"I'm sorry, Tom."

God, look at him. Lying on the floor begging Tom Fallowfield for some shitty forgiveness. Who was Max kidding? No Navy in the whole world would take someone so pathetic, so useless, so—

The sound of Tom's zip coming down was awful. Max screwed up his eyes and mouth and held his breath. He knew what was coming next.

It was hot, vile, and stinking. And when Tom had finished pissing on him, he just zipped up and washed his hands like it was okay. Like it was normal.

Paper rained down on his wet face like confetti.

"Feel free to come back next year," Jazz said, "but that'd be an insult to Tom. And you'd not want to be insulting Tom, right?"

"Right," Max mumbled.

"So knock it off with this options bollocks. And knock it off with this girlfriend shit too, while you're at it."

His heart stopped.

"What?"

"Fat fuckers like you don't get girlfriends, not even crazy ones who think they're boys. So leave her alone, yeah? Anyway, Tom likes blondes. He's going to show her what a real man looks like next time we see her."

Max's heart squeezed tight.

Cian. That sweet little smile in the sea. The shadows and shapes under his T-shirt. The determination to be brave.

"He's not crazy."

"She. Fucking hell, Fatso, you even know what makes a girl a girl? She got a cunt or don't she?"

Max shoved himself to his feet.

"Don't fucking talk about Cian like that!"

The sneer widened. Aidan laughed, barking and hollow in the echoing room.

"Why not, Fatso? She the kind of sicko who spreads her legs for fat—"

Red. In his vision. And on his knuckles. The impact of Jazz's jaw was hard. Harder than any pad or glove in the gym. Harder than the jarring burst of his elbow on Cian's forehead. It shuddered up Max's arm. He heard the crunch. Heard the yowl.

And heard his own trainers squeaking on the tile as he shoved past Jazz and stormed out into the corridor.

He walked into Mr Fraser's classroom, soaking wet and stinking of piss, and said, "Tom Fallowfield's in the toilets, sir. And he's not allowed to be here."

Chapter Twenty-Seven

BY THE TIME Mr Fraser had come back, Max had washed his hair in one of the cavernous sinks in the chemistry lab and dried off laboriously with half of the giant blue toilet roll.

He was still shaking.

It had felt—good.

God, more than good.

He couldn't pull his mind off the wobble and crunch of Jazz's jaw under his fist. And he wanted to do it again. And again and again and again, until Jazz didn't have any teeth left. Until he broke Jazz's jaw, and Jazz couldn't say a single damn thing about Cian ever again.

But by the time Mr Fraser stalked back into the classroom, the reality of what he'd done had started to sink into Max's brain too.

He ratted to a teacher.

He'd never—not once, in all the years he'd been bullied—ratted to a teacher. It only ever made things worse. He hadn't even really told Mum and Aunt Donna about any of it since that first school either. Oh, everyone knew—but Max didn't tell.

But this time, he'd sent Mr Fraser after Tom Fallowfield. On purpose. After punching Jazz in the mouth.

It couldn't get much worse than being pissed on and kicked in the head, but—what if they decided to take it out on Cian instead?

"Fallowfield has been removed from school premises," Mr Fraser said dryly as he strode back in. He was an exceptionally tall, very thin man who looked like he'd been stretched, with long limbs and a long nose to match. He tended to scowl down that nose too. But there was something like bored disinterest on his face as he seated himself opposite Max and steepled his fingers. "I take it there was an altercation?"

Max shrugged, picking at the dried blood on his knuckles.

"I shall simply have to assume, then," Mr Fraser droned. "But may I suggest, Farrier, that you are not so clumsy as to get red paint on your knuckles when Coles is about? People might assume."

Max jumped and glanced up at Mr Fraser's wrinkled, cold face. That dead, reptilian stare bore into him.

"Paint," he echoed faintly. "Um. Yeah. Paint."

"I do believe I saw you earlier today with an art project involving red paint, did I not?"

"Yes, sir," Max said slowly. "Art project. Yeah. Must have...smudged it."

"And where it is now?"

"Binned it, sir. Because I smudged it."

An eyebrow rose, and the faint traces of a smirk lurked on the corners of his mouth. Max stared. Mr Fraser was smiling.

"Uh. You...wanted to see me, sir?"

"Yes. Jack Ryhill informs me that you've put in an options form."

"Uh—"

"And you wish to do chemistry."

Max felt his face heating up.

"Why."

It wasn't a question. It was a demand. A harsh bark of a demand, and Max's face exploded in a blush.

"I—"

Why indeed? He'd just been pissed on by a guy who was half a foot shorter than him. And he'd just lain down and let it happen. Who was he kidding?

"Because," Max said, "I let my boxing instructor and my boyfriend and my Aunt Donna talk this stupid idea into my head that I might actually be able to join the Navy after all. But Jazz is right. I'm nothing but pathetic Fatso Farrier, and I may as well give up on it. So. Sorry to bother you, sir, but I won't be needing a place in your class after all."

"I believe the phrase is 'tough shit,' Farrier."

Max flinched. His eyes flew up to his teacher's impassive, stony face. Mr Fraser swore? But Mr Fraser never swore! He'd once given a kid a month's worth of detention just for saying crap in his class.

"Jeremy Coles has never been right a single day since he stepped into this school," Mr Fraser said sharply. "I take no pleasure in saying it, but the boy is a moron, and his only skill appears to lie in terrorising other children."

"You—you can't call kids stupid," Max blurted out, his shock overriding his survival instincts.

"I think you'll find that I can, Farrier. We teachers do not stop functioning when the gremlins are released from the school. We socialise. We talk. And we talk about our students. So imagine my surprise when Jack Ryhill, hardly your biggest fan, walks into the staffroom one lunchtime and declares that Max Farrier has decided to actually put his nose in his books for a change and sign up for some A-Levels."

Max reddened.

"So why, Farrier, the change of heart?"

"I told you," Max mumbled uncertainly. "I got this crazy idea—"

"That you might actually have some prospects after all?"

Max flinched.

The steepled hands came down. Mr Fraser leaned forward, those cold eyes boring into Max's face like drills.

"Your aunt, your boyfriend, your boxing instructor—they are correct."

Max stared silently back.

"Since you walked into my classroom for the first time, I have watched you deliberately fail every test put in front of you. You're not as clever as you think you are. I know full well you understand my lessons. Nobody naturally makes the errors that you do: you have a tendency, Farrier, to do perfect calculations and then miraculously write the wrong solution."

"I—but—"

"I will not tolerate the same attitude in my A-Level classes."

Max flushed hotly.

"I do not care if you genuinely do not understand something. What I will not tolerate is playing dumb."

"N-no, sir..."

"You will attend every lesson, and you will turn in honest homework and exams. If I even suspect that you are lying to me about your comprehension of a subject, you will be removed from my classes. If you cannot be bothered to put some effort towards your future by then, then I cannot be bothered to waste my time attempting to help you reach it."

"I—I'm sorry, sir."

"You can apologise by performing honestly."

"Yes, sir."

"I understand from Helen Pellow that you wish to follow the family line and go into the Navy?"

"Yes, sir."

"A perfectly fine thing to do," Mr Fraser said quietly and then steepled his fingers again. Peered over the top of them. Stared. "But bear this in mind as well, Farrier. If you put the effort in, you could easily attend university. Not something any of the Farriers—and I taught them all, more fool me—could ever have hoped to have achieved."

Max's jaw sagged.

"You—you taught my dad?"

"From John to George. I taught the lot. And they might have made good sailors, good men, but they were poor students. You have the opportunity to be all three. Don't throw that away."

Max reeled. Be—what? The first Farrier to do a degree? Be more than his dad had been? Be—

Better?

"Yes, sir."

THERE WAS NO training session that evening. Lewis had taken some of the advanced fighters to Birmingham for a competition with another gym, and Cian was at something with the cadets. Max should have been relieved.

But he was antsy instead.

He felt like he had too much energy. He twitched all the way through dinner, and then when he went upstairs with his customary six-pack of Pepsi and packet of biscuits, he found he didn't really want them.

His brain was just too damn loud.

University. Mr Ryhill didn't like him, and Mr Fraser didn't like anyone. But they both thought he ought to go to university. Something his dad had never done. Something no Farrier had ever done. Because they thought he could be even more than his dad, or his Uncle George, or—or Grandpa.

But then—

Yeah. Because Grandpa was ever going to be proud of his grandson who let short boys in Timberlands piss on his head.

Like a degree would ever make up for that.

The thoughts churned and twisted around each other, too loud and too disturbing, and Max found himself changing into his tank top and gym shorts anyway. He couldn't think when he was tired. He couldn't think when his body was screaming at him to stop with the stupid boxing already.

He glanced at himself in the mirror—and paused.

The shorts were...baggy.

His thighs were still swollen balloons of fat. His gut still jutted out like a flabby pregnancy. But—

He could look down and see his enormous feet. And the ankles.

And Cian was right—Aunt Donna was right. He had big feet. Massive feet. The size twelves weren't just fatty size twelves. He could see the arches and the knuckles in his toes. He had big feet.

Squinting at his reflection, thinking of the enormous wall of a man hugging Mum in the old photograph, Max could suddenly see his father looking back at him. His shoulders were obscenely wide, but it wasn't just the fat doing that. He did have enormous hands and feet. Hadn't his hand completely covered Cian's—

Um, okay. Maybe not think of that, if he was going to exercise.

But...there was someone huge under the rolls. The tank top didn't show boobs anymore. The shorts weren't cutting a groove into his belly. But he was still huge.

He was going to be tall. Okay, he was already tall, but—taller.

Big.

Big man, Lewis had called him. He was a big man.

"Fatso Farrier," he said to the reflection, and it didn't sting like it had before.

He turned away and found his water bottle. Walked downstairs. Heard Mum and Aunt Donna talking colour schemes—"I am sick to death of pastel, Lucy!"—and let himself out.

Broke into a jog.

The night was hot, the sun only just sinking below the horizon, and Max kept his head down, staring at those enormous feet as they thumped and thudded on the stinking tarmac. His calves were hard. Hard. They weren't shaking and shuddering like his stomach, they were shifting rocks under skin. The body kicks had done that. The push kicks had done that. And there was something bulging and tough in the way his arms bracketed his chest, something like biceps beginning to peek out from under the rolls.

Why had—

Why had this guy, this guy who was a big man and going to be super tall soon, why had this guy let Tom Fallowfield piss on his head?

Max pounded the pavement until his head hurt, his chest ached, his muscles twinged, and his skin was slick with sweat.

But he didn't find the answer.

Chapter Twenty-Eight

"NO EXAMS, HONEY?"

Max shook his head, busy shovelling breakfast. Aunt Donna had gone to work early, which meant a sneaky fry-up with Mum. And after last night's run, he was really appreciating it.

"No training either?"

Another head shake. Lewis had gone to Birmingham with the advanced class for some competition or other.

"Well, then." Her tone made him look up, and she was giving him that hopeful look. "It's about time we got you measured for your suit."

Shit. "Uh. I should—"

Too late.

Max hated buying clothes at the best of times—having to shop in the triple XL range when you were a teenager was just humiliating—but Mum was having things tailor-made. And have a measuring tape applied around his gut? No way. It would take, like, a year's more running to make that acceptable.

But...Mum did that thing where she made her eyes wide and looked at him all hurt and hopeful, and it always felt really shitty to say no when she did that. So Max sucked it up and grumbled an agreement.

Still—

It wasn't all bad. He rarely got Mum to himself these days, and Aunt Donna had taken the car, so walking down to the harbour in the morning sun with Mum was not only necessary but a bit of a treat. She was pretty, Max's mum. She still turned heads, and it felt nice to walk down to the seafront without thinking the heads were turning to goggle at him for once. And she was giggly and happy, just the way Max loved her the most, as they made fun of his Uncle George's RSVP for the wedding, insisting he needed a plus-one space but not being able to so much as name the girl he'd be bringing with him.

"I'm glad he's coming, though," Mum admitted as they reached the boutique bridal store, tucked away in a narrow side street, the cobbles gleaming in the sunlight. "John's given some weak excuse."

The shop bell jingled over their heads. Movement rustled in the back, and then a plump woman with a big smile and bigger hair swept in, and beamed.

"Lucy! There you are, my love—and this must be Max."

Max squirmed.

"A full tuxedo is it? Let's have a look—oh, men's section for you, dear, definitely, look at these shoulders! Lucy, dear, I think we'll make him a size too large. He'll never still be this height by the big day." One minute Max was at the door, and the next, he was on a stool in a back room, with Ada and a skinny little rake of an assistant putting tape measures everywhere. Why the hell did he need his wrists measured for a suit? And she talked a mile a minute about give and seams and silk linings and the colour blue—

"Aunt Donna's right," he told Mum. "This is way too complicated. I'm never going to get married."

Mum laughed. "Well, I didn't get a proper wedding the first time, so you can both like it or lump it."

"Why not?" Max asked curiously.

She waved a hand airily. "I was a pregnant teenager living in my boyfriend's parents' house because mine were so angry with me over the whole thing. We got married in a registry office, and my white dress was an off-the-rail summer dress from Debenhams."

Ada tittered. "Ooh, could have been worse, dear. My old mum got married in her funeral skirt!"

Max stared as the women swapped wedding horror stories, and a whole book of numbers were taken off him. When he was finally allowed to step down, he was made to stand at a wall and have six million fabric samples held up against him—all the same shade of grey, but with different names—while Mum picked.

Honestly, if this was what people had to do to get married, he'd take the registry office.

"I bet Dad didn't have to wear a tux," he grumbled, and Mum rolled her eyes.

"He wore his dress uniform if you must know. And don't you start, I'm still convinced Donna's going to show up in her overalls and boots."

"It would be memorable?" Max attempted but was overridden by three women snorting in unison.

"Dear, that attitude is why the women have to handle these things," Ada said and shoved a pile of fabric in his hands. "Men. Honestly! Now go and put that on, go on, through there. Lucy! Lucy, dear, have you made a decision on that dress? We're going to need a decision soon, you know—"

Max pulled the curtain shut behind him and shook out the suit. And...the accessories. Okay. So. What was supposed to go where?

His phone buzzed while he was attempting to work out something that looked like Cian's binder, and the devil himself was texting.

Help! Max replied. *Mum's got me trying on wedding suits and I have no idea what goes where!*

You knew just fine what went where the other weekend ;) came the totally useless reply.

Sex is easier than suits, Max opined and got a string of laughing emojis for his distress. *Seriously, rescue me, this is terrifying.*

Fine, fine. Where are you, O Damsel in Distress?

The bridal boutique down by the harbour.

Ok, five minutes. I'm babysitting, and Katie likes chucking rocks at the seagulls.

Max rolled his eyes and dropped the phone on the chair, going back to the mirror and the weird black binder thing. Where the hell was it supposed to go? What even was it? Screw it. Let Ada laugh. He was never getting married.

He rejected the bow tie outright—not happening, no way, not ever—but grudgingly decided the waistcoat did look kind of sophisticated. And...yeah. Shoulders. They barely fit in the frame of the mirror, and the waistcoat and his upper arms made him look...

Built.

Not fat. Built.

Max plucked at the fabric and frowned critically. He looked...okay. Like. Not awesome. But okay. Ish.

"Max, dear, you all right in there?"

He sighed. Fine.

"There's too much random stuff," he said and pulled back the curtain.

Mum froze.

She was standing up on the stool he'd been placed on, her flowery top and dungarees replaced by a voluminous white dress—but she was staring at him, eyes wide.

And watery.

"Um. Mum?"

"Oh, Max."

He shifted on his feet—and then recoiled in horror as she burst into tears.

"Mum!"

"Oh, I'm sorry, I'm sorry, I'm sorry, I just—come here. Come here, come here..."

He stumbled forward and let her stoop to hug him, the wedding dress scratchy and uncomfortable between them. She sobbed on his shoulder for a minute, and Max racked his brains for what to do. What was he supposed to do? Since when did wearing a stupid suit make Mum cry?

"Um." He patted her shoulder hesitantly. "It's—okay?"

"I'm sorry," she sniffled, pushing him to arm's length and visibly pulling herself together. "You just look—oh, you look wonderful, darling."

"Um. Thanks?"

"You do," she insisted, wiping her nose on the back of her hand.

"Ew, Mum." He found her a tissue from her handbag.

"Give over," she mumbled and blew her nose noisily. "You look—God, when did my little Max turn into you, eh?"

He reddened. "Mum!" Thankfully, Ada and the skinny one had tactfully withdrawn to somewhere else in the shop.

"No, I'm allowed, this is a parent thing, you wouldn't understand," she said, swatting at him. Then she stroked his hair and beamed. "You're going to look wonderful. Even your grandpa would be getting teary right about now."

Max grunted, shifting uncomfortably.

"Max?"

He glanced up. Well. At. Even on the stool, Mum was only an inch or two taller than him.

"Are you...okay?"

"Um. Yeah?"

"With this, I mean?"

"No. I hate suits. They're uncomfortable and—"

"No, no, I mean...the wedding, darling."

Max blinked at her. She was biting her lip anxiously. And it looked all wrong. She was in a wedding dress. She should be giggly and happy, like when they'd come in.

"Yeah," he said. "Why wouldn't I be?"

"You...you just don't seem...that enthused about it."

He shifted. "Yeah, well, I'm not really interested in weddings and stuff..."

"And you still call Donna your aunt."

Max winced. "Oh."

"If—if there's a problem, Max..."

"It's a force of habit," he said. "You know, she's...Aunt Donna. And I can't exactly call her my mum, can I? You're Mum."

She squeezed his shoulders, and he shut up.

"Honey. I love her. I love her very much, and she makes me happy. But—you have to know, if it came down to a choice, if you really weren't okay with this—you'd win. If it had to be you or her, it would be you. You know that, don't you? You're the most important person in the world to me."

A lump formed in Max's throat. Savage. Hard. His eyes blurred, and his face was hot.

He coughed.

Swallowed.

"I know, Mum."

She hugged him. Her hair was soft against his face, and her perfume familiar. He squeezed tight, as though trying to memorise her. His earliest memories were right here. Her perfume and the way she hugged him.

He sniffed, hard, and dragged it all back together.

"You're being stupid," he said.

"Am I?"

"Yeah. There's no me or Donna thing."

"No?"

"No. I like her fine. She's cool. You know—scary. But cool."

Mum chuckled and pulled back. She'd cried again, but she smiled again too.

"You're really all right with this?"

Max shrugged. "She's fine. And you're happy since she came along. So yeah. I mean, you know, don't tell her. She'll be all smug and insufferable."

Mum laughed. Max grinned. Job done. He hated it when Mum got all watery. It only reminded him of being little and finding her crying every family occasion that Dad wasn't there for anymore.

"And I'm not okay with having to wear this tuxedo thing. It's awful. What's the stupid binder thing even for?" he asked, warming to his theme, and Ada swept back in as though nothing had happened.

"Tsh, you need lessons, young man," she scolded. "Arms up. Yes, yes—Trisha! Add a centimetre or two to the sleeves. As I thought—you're all out of proportion, dear. Look at these arms..."

Naturally, when Max was standing there in a horrible, half-constructed tuxedo with a skinny woman shoving a tape measure into his armpit and arguing with her supervisor about extra centimetres—*naturally*, that was when the bell jingled, and Cian walked in.

"Oh," he said and grinned. "Nice."

"Shut up," Max said.

Mum laughed. "Hello, Cian, darling. Come to have a look at our Max in his finest, have you?"

"That's not his finest," Cian said meaningfully, and Max flushed.

"Shut up," he insisted.

Katie, hanging off her brother's hand, told him that 'shut up' wasn't nice, and then turned to Mum, eyed her up and down, and decried the dress as too 'floofy.'

"Sorry, Mrs Farrier. Someone is grumpy because she's not allowed to eat ice cream until she's sick," Cian said, rolling his eyes.

"Well, I sympathise. It's one of life's pleasures," Mum said haughtily and then waved a hand at Max. "Go on, darling, go and have some fun. In fact, go and get yourselves lunch. There's a twenty in my purse."

Max dived back into the cubicle to change, face burning as he heard Katie loudly ask what his finest was. Thankfully, he didn't hear the reply.

When he emerged, Mum was holding up another dress against herself and busy arguing with Ada about the merits of it against the one she had on. Max filched the twenty, turned Cian around, and escaped.

The moment the door closed behind them, he called Cian unhelpful and said he'd been enjoying that far too much.

"Hm, let's see, you in a waistcoat? Yeah. I enjoyed that."

Max grumbled. He didn't want to like the stupid suit, but— "Didn't know you had a thing for waistcoats."

"Neither did I until five minutes ago."

They got jacket potatoes in a cafe, barely talking due to Cian needing to patiently make up lies about why the sky was blue but clouds were white. But when they ventured back outside, Katie became preoccupied with trying to catch seagulls, and Max found himself sitting on the harbour wall, arm around Cian's hip, and a faint layer of sweat building under his arms.

He could just...

Lean in. Turn. Stop talking about exams and the upcoming wedding, and—

So he did.

Cian made a pleased sound—when had Max learned the meaning of those individual noises?—and a hand curled into the cotton of Max's T-shirt. Max's hand curled inwards from hip and found arse. Balance. Politeness. Just helping. It'd hurt if they fell off, so yeah. He was duty-bound to put it there.

There was a sharp blow to his leg and he yelped.

"Cian! Stop being disgusting!" Katie yelled.

Cian cackled. "Never!"

"I'll tell Mum!"

"You go ahead," he jeered. "I'll just do it again, watch."

Max laughed into the kiss, Katie hitting them again and yowling in six-year-old horror. She even decided they'd get cooties, which Max hadn't thought kids really did.

Then, when Cian dropped off the wall to grab her and turn her upside down, Max found himself staring across the harbour.

And Jazz Coles was staring right back.

The hairs on the back of Max's neck prickled. The sweat was suddenly cold.

"Max?"

He jumped. Stared down at Cian. He'd dropped Katie, who'd run after another seagull, and was staring up at Max, frowning.

"You okay?"

Max nodded across the harbour.

Cian looked—and smirked. "Ah," he said and then stepped forward.

Right between Max's legs.

"What's he going to do?" Cian whispered. "Your mum's like two hundred feet away. There's a whole bunch of shoppers. And we have a kid who can kick for Britain."

Max swallowed.

"He'll come after you. He knows what you are."

"Let him. He'll find out in short order what I'm not, too."

"What's that?"

"Weak," Cian said and grinned. "I'll crack his skull open from ear to ear."

Max coughed. "Uh. He might have said some stuff about you, and I might have...decked him."

"You decked him?"

"Yeah."

"Proper cross?"

"Proper cross."

"How hard?"

"Uh. Might have...loosened a tooth or two."

"Mm, not bad. We'll have to work on that, though."

"Work on it?"

Why was Cian so close, yet still talking?

"Yeah. Next time, I fully expect you to break his jaw."

"Just to defend your honour?"

He was right there.

"Yeah. That's it. My honour."

Max licked his lips. Cian's gaze flickered down.

"It's only proper," Max murmured. "Can't have him talking smack about my boyfriend."

Cian grinned. "Right. So—"

Fuck it.

Max cupped that pale, freckled face in both hands and kissed him.

Said everything he wanted to, right there. Said everything he felt, right there. In the sun. Joined like they could never be parted. The sea rumbling beyond the wall. Gulls screaming in the air.

Katie's sharp little shoe smacked him in the leg again, but Max didn't stop.

If he could do this forever—just this, right here, forever—then he would.

Chapter Twenty-Nine

MRS WILLIAMS CAME to get Katie at four.

"But I don't want to go to ballet!" the entire town was informed at the top of Katie's lungs, and Cian pulled a face.

"I'll get the bus back," he said. "Enjoy the noise."

The look his mother threw him could have turned milk, and Max sniggered as she drove off.

"I don't think she's your biggest fan right now," he said.

"Wait 'til Katie tells her how many Starbursts I let her have." Cian shuffled a little closer on the wall. "So."

Max put his hand on Cian's back pocket. Manners and all that.

"So," he echoed.

"How about..."

Cian's fingers were caught in the neck of Max's T-shirt. Toying with his skin. Despite the heat, Max could feel goosebumps rising in their wake.

"...you and me..."

Cian's sunburn had morphed into a new layer of freckles, and there was one right by his lower lip. Like, touching it. Max's tongue itched to touch it too.

"...go somewhere quiet and play a game?"

"What kind of game?"

Cian's eyebrows jumped up his face. "I dunno," he whispered—and then grinned. Broke the spell. "Hide the sausage?"

Max burst out laughing. Cian yelped as they nearly overbalanced and then laughed and clung to Max's shoulders, sniggering into his neck. Hot and warm and right there—

Oh hell, the spell was back.

"You said next time we'd need a hot tub."

"Mm, good point. Could hide it somewhere else, though?"

Max's fingers skittered in shock on Cian's arse.

"Uh—really?"

"Sure."

Max swallowed, throat dry. "Um. Yeah. Okay. Yeah. Uh—"

Cian laughed. He was all sun-white hair and bright blue eyes, made of muscle on a wire frame inside his combat cut-offs and tight T-shirt. Max wanted them gone. Wanted Cian. All of him. All of the time too.

"This isn't fair," he complained.

"What's not?"

"I get all dumb and flustered when you're around, and you don't."

Cian snorted. "Uh, yes I do."

Max eyed him sceptically.

"What?" Cian asked, shrugging. He slid his fingers through Max's hair, spiking it up, and the grin widened. "My interest just isn't as visible as yours. Trust me. If you had your hands in the right places, you'd know about it."

Max's brain stalled.

"Uh—"

"Wanna feel it?"

"Um. Yes. Yes. But—you don't—it makes you feel—"

"Let me worry about that," Cian said and tugged on his hair. "So? You want to stay here and have some PG-13 fun, or do you want to take this somewhere more private?"

"Uh—"

"Well, a bit. I quite like getting you to come undone in public."

"You could skip 'undone' and it'd still work," Max groused and Cian laughed.

Kissed the corner of his lip.

Placed Max's hands on the bare crook of Cian's knee.

"Come on, Max." The wheedle in his ear was breathy, delicate, and pure sex. "Let's go and play."

Max gulped. Oh, God.

"All right, lovebirds?"

His heart stopped.

The cry was like a bucket of ice water over the head. His lungs seized up. His hands clutched tight at Cian's waist. And he couldn't breathe.

Cian could, though. The heavy sigh and magnificent eye-roll spoke of no such issues. He pulled back. Glanced idly down from the wall. Sneered a "What?" as though answering an annoying child.

Jazz sneered right back.

"That's really nice, that. Here we are, saying hello—"

"Yeah, hi, now piss off," Cian said.

The sneer deepened into a scowl.

"You're as rude as he is," Jazz snapped.

"I'm not the one interrupting a private conversation," Cian returned. "Why don't you lot naff off and leave us in peace, yeah?"

Jazz snorted. Tom, at his right shoulder, gave Cian's legs a very visible once-over.

"Nice legs," he said.

"Thanks. Go away."

"I don't mind a girl who doesn't shave."

The next eye-roll threatened to pop something. "How very progressive of you." Somewhere in the back of Max's frozen brain, he registered something.

Cian could sneer worse than Jazz.

Damn.

"Tom's good with girls," Jazz snapped. "Maybe you ought to try a real man."

"Got one. Cheers for the tip. Shove it."

"What, Fatso Farrier? What's he got?" Jazz sniggered.

Cian disengaged. His hands crept back. He turned on the wall. Leaned forward.

And his eyes narrowed in a way that Max recognised from Jazz himself.

A predator. That had seen prey. And was homing in fast.

Completely inappropriately, Max's blood thawed and began to head south.

"What's he got?" Cian echoed softly. "Depends what we're measuring against. You about to tell me that Boots here has got a ten-inch dick and all the girls love it?"

Jazz's eyes narrowed in reply.

"What, you like fat cock, do you?"

Cian smiled.

No.

Beamed.

"Oh, I dunno..."

The movement was so fast, so sharp, so clean, that Max almost missed it.

No part of Cian's body moved except his right knee. One minute, it was bent, both trainers flat against the wall—and the next, the knee was straight.

The trainer—pointed, perfect, a ballet-worthy angle— struck Jazz with an audible *thud*.

Jazz howled.

Doubled. Collapsed. Clutching at his groin with an animalistic agony.

"He's definitely got better than you," Cian finished sweetly and then turned cold blue eyes on Tom and Aidan. "Wanna try a ride, boys? Tell you what. If you can touch the button on my shorts, you can have 'em off. Wanna try that?"

Aidan backed off. Eyeing Jazz. Frowning.

But Tom snarled and started forwards.

And Cian shoved off the wall with a yell. Just—flew. Dived. Shot off it like it was a launch pad.

Max knew what he was going to do long before he did it.

He'd jumped high. Legs out straight behind him. One fist up, by his face. Guarding. The other arm bent in half. The shoulder rolled. The elbow came up. High. Straight.

And down.

The crack was like a gunshot. They crashed to the ground, Cian nearly bouncing up again, shaking out a bloodied elbow with a manic grin and wide blue eyes. Tom—did not.

Tom stayed down.

And bellowed.

"Fuck," Max breathed—and jumped. He leapt down and seized Cian's wrist. Pulled. People were staring. There was going to be trouble. And then, when Jazz stopped nursing his 'nads, there was going to be more trouble.

"Oi! You two!"

"Leg it!" Max hissed.

Blood was streaked up Cian's arm—and over the cobbles, over Tom's face, everywhere. Tom was still yelling. People were starting to run over.

So Max pulled.

And they ran.

And near enough a half mile later, in the crooked side streets and shadows of the approaching evening, Max lunged. Caught both arms around Cian's waist and lifted him, small as a doll, delicate and tiny.

Slammed him up against a wall and caught his grinning mouth with Max's own.

Cian clutched back, all limbs and laughter, hard. Strong. Powerful.

Max's.

"Let's go to mine," Max breathed between their faces, breathless with the run and some kind of strange euphoria in his veins. "Fuck, they'll kill us. Fuck it. Fuck it. I wanna—"

Cian laughed.

"Fuck." He squeezed his thighs tight around Max's waist. "Yeah. Sounds good. Then later? When they come to kill us? I'll just kill 'em all over again."

"THAT WAS AMAZING," Max whispered, awed.

Cian laughed, stretched out beside him in the grass. "Thank you?"

"Not that."

"Oh."

"Though that was too."

"Nice save," Cian said and rolled over. He propped himself up on his elbow, grinning. "So? What was so amazing?"

"You."

"When?"

"I don't know," Max said sarcastically. "When you kicked Jazz so hard he'll never have kids. And when you split Tom's skull like an egg."

"I didn't break him," Cian chided and then chuckled. "I'm not heavy enough. And it'd break my arm to try."

"It was still amazing."

"Thanks."

Max rolled over too and craned his neck for a kiss. Cian smelled of them, and Max lingered, nose against one thin cheek, to breathe.

"You know," Cian whispered, "if you'd try it once in a while, they'd be less of an issue."

"What?"

"Kicking some balls and elbowing some faces."

"They wouldn't," Max said. "Told you, I loosened one of Jazz's teeth."

"Uh-huh. Had they beaten you up before then?"

Max swallowed.

"That's a yes, then."

"Yeah," he mumbled.

"Did you see the weaselly one?"

The switch threw him. "What?"

"The one who didn't talk."

"Aidan?"

"If that's his name."

"No, why?"

"I kicked your mate Jazz-Hands and he backed off. Aidan, that is. He didn't want to try."

"Tom did though. And Tom's the real problem."

"Tom has a real problem. It's three inches long and going to need stitches."

Max laughed and kissed him again.

"Seriously though," Cian murmured there, soft and sweet. "Don't wait next time. Don't make it about me. Next time—just go for broke."

The cold ball of fear in Max's gut tightened.

"I can't," he breathed. "They'll kill me."

"Sure," Cian said and grinned. "Like three fishing boats taking on the *Bulwark*. Don't try that one, big man. You got this. You just keep telling yourself you don't."

Max opened his mouth—

And closed it.

"I got this," he murmured to himself.

"Yup. And hey—" Cian wriggled, naked in the grass, and successfully ruined any chance Max had at coherent thought. "—Lewis will be back tomorrow. And he texted me this morning."

"About what?"

"About you."

"Me?"

"Uh-huh."

"What about me?"

"Oh, you'll see," Cian said and turned over. Stretched. Completely and utterly naked, save for his T-shirt arranged carefully over his—shapes.

Max stared.

"If you do everything Lewis says tomorrow," Cian said, staring resolutely at the sky, "then I'll let you."

"Uh. Let me. Let me—what?"

"Look."

"Uh."

"And if you do it well," Cian said, turning back over and kissing Max full on the mouth, "then I'll even let you touch."

Lewis had to have something awful planned.

But...yeah. Power of boners.

So Max said, "Okay."

And knew that, whatever it was, Cian would make it worth it.

Chapter Thirty

"GRADING."

What.

"No," Max said.

Cian stretched both arms over his head and stuck his hips out until his spine creaked.

"Bastard," Max muttered.

"What?"

"Nothing. Nothing..."

"You're ready. They're ready. So. In you go," Lewis said, jabbing a finger at the main gym door. "Get graded. Get your armband. And get back out here."

"No."

"You stop training with us in two weeks, Max. After that, you can do whatever you want."

"I can do whatever I want in here!"

"Sure you can," Lewis said. "But a deal's a deal. You grade, or no reference."

Max's chest seized.

No reference. Oh crap, he'd forgotten all about it. Between the school form and exams and Jazz and Tom and Cian—God, Cian—he'd totally forgotten the deal.

And—two weeks?

Was that all he had left?

"Grading. Go."

Max opened his mouth. Protested. Looked at Lewis's impassive face.

Looked at Cian's. And his body. All long and lean and stretched out. With the pink lines from swimming naked and—

Max swallowed.

Okay. So....

Tonight, he could see. If he did what Lewis said.

Only that was a class full of fit students grading, and Max was—

Broad shoulders. Big feet. Extra centimetres because he was growing all over the place. Going to...going to do A-Levels. Maybe university. The Navy.

He sucked in a breath—and his gut—and turned. Pushed on the door. Heard it swing shut behind him.

Heads turned.

His stomach rolled sickeningly.

And—the heads turned back to the front. He slipped into a gap, already sweating.

And up at the front, Josh beamed.

"All right," he said. "That's everyone. Let's do this."

Max was dying.

He was convinced of it. Lying flat on his back and staring at the eaves, he was going to die. Right here. With his chest exploding, his legs on fire, and every last thought coming back around to a simple, singular conclusion.

Fuck Aunt Donna.

In fact—as he reeled in more oxygen past a rasping throat and into spasming lungs—fuck Lewis too. Lewis had made him do this. And fuck Cian for standing by and not helping. Max was going to die, right here, right now, because of the three of them.

Out of the corner of his eye, he saw feet.

Then knees.

"All right, kid?"

He gurgled uselessly. Josh chuckled.

"You really put the work in there."

Work? Sure. Had it worked? N—

"Congratulations."

"W-what?" Max spluttered.

"You heard."

Max squinted at Josh's face. He was smiling. Not smirking. Just—smiling.

"I passed?"

"Sure did."

"Like—I scraped it, or—?"

"Nope. Flying colours. Heck, that elbow strike on its own would have taken you over the top."

Max's arm throbbed in memory.

As many push-ups as possible in a minute. As many sit-ups as possible in another minute. As many burpees, a third minute. Then a bleep test. Then demonstrate every move on command to some invisible opponent. Then spar with Josh for three minutes.

And then die, in Max's opinion, because that was just ridiculous.

He'd wobbled and sweated his way through it all. His hands were so slick that the gloves had nearly come off. He'd not landed a single punch, and Josh's push kick had broken through Max's guard and nearly made him hurl.

"But—" he panted. "I didn't even do ten push-ups."

"Uh-huh. How many could you do when you started?"

Max opened his mouth.

Oh.

"Two," he admitted. And that had been through sheer force of will, not...well, actual ability.

"Next grading, you have to do more than you did today," Josh said, shrugging. "Same for the other exercises. Just beat your last grading every time. That's it."

That's it, he said. While Max was drowning in a puddle of sweat on the floor.

"I—passed?"

"Yep. Come to the front desk once you've had a drink and a shower, and we'll get you your armband."

With that, he was gone. Max levered himself up on his sore elbows and watched as Josh padded across to a girl with a long rope of blonde hair in a plait and began to talk to her. She had an armband already, a woven pattern of cloth that looked kind of like a weird friendship bracelet for the bicep.

Did—did Max get one of those?

Something weird and tense unfurled in his chest.

He'd done it.

He'd passed. He'd succeeded. He'd not done a Fatso Farrier Failure. He'd nearly died, but he'd done it.

His stomach clenched.

Heaving himself to his feet—and then bracing his hands on his knees to prevent himself from falling over at the shriek of pain in his thighs—Max found himself peering down his sweaty legs to those boat-sized feet, bare as baby whales on the mats. Big feet. Big man.

Not fat feet.

Not fat man.

He'd done it. He'd graded.

Everything hurt—from feet to face—but he'd done it. He had something to show for these months of torture. He had something to be pro—

Max swallowed.

Pride.

He'd forgotten what it felt like to be proud.

But the thumping in his chest and the dizzying sense of euphoria that was starting to rub out the pain was unmistakeably that.

Slowly, he shuffled towards the doors. He'd taken so long to drag himself out of the training room that the shower bank was completely free, and by the time he'd limped out again, the other boys had long gone. Except for one.

Cian was sitting on the bench, playing with Max's phone.

"What are you—"

"Levelling you up on *Candy Crush*," Cian drawled and then grinned up at him. "Just drip-dry there for us, yeah?"

Max scowled.

"I nearly died in there."

"Sure."

"I could have had a heart attack."

"Uh-huh."

"I could have drowned in my own sweat."

"If you weren't going to drown yourself in that shower, I doubt the sweat would have helped." Cian beamed. "So. Josh might have mentioned something about an armband."

"Yeah."

"You passed, then?"

"Uh. Yeah. Yeah, I guess so."

"You guess?"

"I don't pass stuff, okay? It's...weird."

"Why?"

Max coughed a laugh. "Fatso Farrier always fails."

And yet it didn't sting. It sounded...almost like a joke. Almost funny. Because of course he didn't always fail. He could see his feet, and he was drip-drying in front of his boyfriend. He'd passed a grading. He was—

"Funny," Cian said, smirking. "Fatso Farrier looks like he's doing pretty okay from where I'm sitting."

Max pulled a face. Cian just pulled one right back and bit his lip.

"Is your stepmum picking you up?"

"Not 'til I text her."

"How about you don't text her."

Max blinked.

"You deserve a reward," Cian said and stood up. Began to shrug out of his jacket. "And I know you've wanted a look. So—one time only deal. You can have thirty seconds. Thirty seconds to do whatever you want." The T-shirt came off. "Then they go away, and you'll have to find some way of earning another thirty seconds."

Max's lungs closed up for a totally different reason.

The bra hit the floor.

"Oh," Max said.

Um. Well. Shape. And shadow. Only—yeah, well, no shadows under the bright glare of the halogen lights. They were just—there. All of a sudden. Small and soft, and—

Max's palms itched. Both to touch, and with the memory of the one and only time he'd been allowed to touch them before. Thirty seconds. He could touch in thirty seconds. Feel them again. Remember.

But then he curled his hands into fists.

No way could he not look, but—Cian didn't like them. Didn't like Max seeing them or touching them. This was—this was, like, the biggest gift Cian could give. Right up there with that Saturday morning in the sea. This was Cian being brave.

Because Max had been brave and done the grading.

So Max squeezed his fists until he felt the knuckles aching and stared as though he could burn the image of them into the backs of his eyeballs.

Then Cian stooped and picked up the bra.

Covered them up.

Shrugged back into his T-shirt.

His face was a little pink, and Max swallowed thickly.

"Thank you," he mumbled.

"You were doing your stare again."

"What stare?"

"The one where it's like you want to bite me."

Max coughed. "Might have occurred to me."

Cian laughed and his shoulders eased. The jacket was shrugged back on without a trace of unhappiness.

"It's nice," he said quietly. "Does that make it weird? That I want you to look at me like that, even though I hate why?"

"Um, I don't know if you've noticed," Max said, "but I stare at your legs like that too, and those aren't exactly girly."

The next laugh was higher. Sweeter.

Better, and Max could taste it when Cian kissed him. Taste mirth and relief.

"Thanks," he whispered against Cian's lips and then shoved.

"Hey!"

"I'm too tired for you!"

"Oh whatever," Cian mocked. "Come on. Let's go and get your armband. Too tired to walk up to the field?"

"Yes," Max said emphatically.

No, said his body.

Chapter Thirty-One

IT WAS OVER.

That had been Lewis's deal in the end. Max had passed the grading. So he didn't have to go anymore.

So why, the following evening, did he find himself staring at the ceiling, at his ships racing across the white plaster sky, and simply counting the breaths in his lungs?

He felt—twitchy.

He'd been revising all day—the last of his exams were coming up over the next fortnight, and then he'd be free—and usually after dinner, Aunt Donna would give him that look, and he'd grumble all the way into the van and all the way to the gym.

But tonight, he'd just shuffled back up to his room, and she'd stayed downstairs to argue seating plans with Mum.

So Max found himself staring at the ceiling and counting his breaths.

He felt—unwell, almost. The steak and kidney pie was sitting heavy in his gut. It felt like it was stretching him. His fingers were restless, twitching on the sheets in time to soundless music, and every rake of air—in, out, in again— too sharp and too painful inside his chest.

He wanted to move.

It was a weird feeling, and Max didn't know what to do with it. He was done boxing. He didn't have to go and get smacked around anymore. And even if he wanted to go back—which he didn't—Aunt Donna wasn't going to keep paying for the private lessons. He'd have to go into the main class. With all the others.

It wouldn't just be him and Cian anymore, which had been the only good thing about it, so why the hell was he wondering what time the bus out to the industrial estate was?

"Stop it," he told himself. "You can have your life back now."

No more training. No more sweating to death. No more being tortured by Lewis—torture sanctioned by his own stepmother-to-be. None of it. He was free. He could eat what he wanted, do what he wanted, go where he wanted.

So he was lying on his bed. Drumming the mattress with his fingers. And staring at his ships like they had personally insulted him.

Christ, what was the matter with him?

He didn't want to watch a film. He couldn't text Cian, because Cian would be training. More than ever now—he had his instructor's course coming up. Mum and Aunt Donna were brewing up a storm downstairs, so offering to help would probably only get him yelled at. And just staring at the ceiling was making Max feel antsy—as though he was jumping out of his own skin.

He had to move.

Slowly, he heaved himself off the bed. Staring down at his bare feet, he eyed the lines of muscle in his calves. His ankles. The shadows of his shins. Where had everything gone?

The mirror didn't help find it. His thighs were like tree trunks—massive, but hard. His stomach was still a roll of fat shoving out his shirt like a pregnancy, but his shoulders were bursting out of the sleeves for an entirely different reason. The neckline gaped open, sagging and misshapen. His chin—well, there was a chin. Not five of them. And his arms, when he experimentally curled his hands into pudgy fists, rippled and hardened into ropes. His shirt strained.

Fatso Farrier stared into the mirror, and a big man stared right back.

In more than one sense. His sweatpants weren't covering his ankles anymore. The hem of his T-shirt didn't quite touch the waistband.

By the time school started again, he'd be back to himself. Back to the lardy lad in Year Twelve. Back to double packets of digestives and six-packs of Pepsi. This humming in his veins, this weird energy he couldn't shake, would be gone.

And Max frowned.

He didn't want Aunt Donna to win, but...he didn't want to go back either.

He didn't want several days of torture in the gym a week, but—

But Fatso Farrier hadn't put in his options form. Fatso Farrier hadn't graded yesterday. Fatso Farrier didn't have a reference from his boxing instructor for the Navy. Max had.

Fatso Farrier got pissed on by Tom Fallowfield in the boys' toilets. Max didn't.

And Max didn't want to be Fatso Farrier anymore.

Slowly, Max turned away from the mirror—and reached for his sports bag.

IT WAS COOL. There was a fine, misty rain that had rolled in off the sea. Max's T-shirt was sticking to him, and his calves were howling in pain by the time he stopped running.

And he stopped at the bottom of the hill.

He'd been running for an hour, but Cian wouldn't be home. There was nobody Max wanted to see at the cottages on their tiny, darkened lane.

But the hill stretched out above him. Like a challenge. Like a dare.

He'd never run it. Limped it. Staggered it. Even walked it, once or twice. But never run.

And there was that humming in his veins. He'd been running for an hour, but he was still restless. If he ran up the hill—

Max raked a deep breath past aching ribs and lumbered forward. One wet trainer in front of the other. His calves stretched uncomfortably. His shoulders hunched up, before he forced them down. Run straight. Run tall. Lewis had taught him that. Scrunching up hurt, was inefficient, made it worse. Run tall.

Big men especially should always run tall.

The first ten yards hurt. The next ten were worse. The third gave him a stitch. The fourth defeated the run and turned into a wildly veering jog. His thighs ached. His shins felt like they were breaking. All Max could do was gasp—in, in, in, in—as his shoes slid and squeaked against the damp, dirty track.

As he rose.

Rose out of the town and up the hill.

It was exposed, where the old road gave up the ghost and turned into nothing more than a muddy track. The wind caught at his hair and tugged the damp curls into rough spikes at the back of his neck. The misty rain was full now. Drops slithered down his back—sweat or seawater, he couldn't tell. There was salt in the air. A heavy oppression had lifted.

And the track was levelling. The lights from the cottages were like tiny suns in the blackness of space.

Max gulped at thin air and turned around.

Below him, the town glittered. Beyond it, the sea. He could see flashes of lightning on the horizon, far away and unfurling above the ocean.

He breathed.

He'd run to the top of the hill—and still, still, there was something raw and powerful in his veins. Something sweet in the aching in his ribs and legs. Something big.

Max curled up his fists next to his chest and peered downwards. Downhill was easy. It would be downhill all the way home from here. Another forty minutes of running if he ran properly. If he put the effort in.

He could never have done this sixteen weeks ago.

"Okay," he gasped. Squeezed his fists tighter. Relaxed his shoulders.

And ran.

Chapter Thirty-Two

HIS PHONE BEEPED the minute Max switched it back on.

You, me, back row, bad movie. Y/Y?

He grinned.

He hadn't seen Cian since grading. He hadn't been back to the gym either. And apart from a couple of texts over the weekend, which were mostly Cian whining about babysitting duty and Max whining about wedding planning, there hadn't been anything going on.

Max missed him. Both simply missed him—the company, the fun, that little thrill that someone like Cian wanted to be with someone like Max—but also, in a far more basic and primal way, he missed the feel of Cian's mouth.

Yes, he replied. *Just leaving my exam. Where are you?*

At home, came the swift reply. *Let me get an ETA.*

There was a brief pause, while Max shoved his stuff in his bag and followed the crowd of chattering students out of the building and across the grass towards the side entrance. Then—

Mum says I have to get the bus because she's a witch.

Your mum is amazing.

WITCH. See you in about 20?

I'll go get tickets, Max offered and was firmly told that musicals would see him single again. Grinning, he pocketed the phone. What did Cian care if he picked some shitty musical? They wouldn't be watching it anyway.

The heatwave had broken over the weekend, but it was coming back with a vengeance. Town stank. Everyone was crowded into the shadowy, narrow side streets, desperate for a reprieve from the sun, and so Max found himself sticking to shop windows and doorways and creeping along in the little shade left behind. Seagulls strutted down the middle of the high street, lording it over their new kingdom.

Bad movie and then maybe go home. Mum was out with her girlfriends tonight, and Aunt Donna always took the excuse to turn up the TV really loud and watch Formula One or something else with lots of explosions and crashes. She'd not bother them if Max and Cian just sort of...stole away upstairs. Back row in the cinema always got Cian in a sort of handsy mood, Max had learned, and Max felt that their run of luck in not getting caught at it in public was going to run out sooner or later. And—

"Oi, Fatso!"

He stopped.

Despite the heat, a prickle of cold shot up his spine.

New shadows formed around him. Boots wandered into his view of the dry, hot pavement. Timberlands.

Max balled his hands into fists. Really? *Really?* He—he had plans. Good plans. He'd done well on his paper. He was going to see a bad film with his boyfriend. Why did he have to run into them?

"Come on, Fatso." An elbow dug into his side. "Come with us."

"Where?" Max asked.

"Just come on."

Jazz's voice was deceptively calm. Almost friendly. Nobody would bat an eyelash. Which, Max suspected, was rather the point.

"Where?" he repeated.

"Don't be difficult, Farrier. Come on."

A hand closed around his elbow, and he jerked it free.

"No need for that."

"What do you want?" he persisted.

"We want to talk. So come on. Somewhere quieter."

Max eyed the empty street. The shoppers were packed into air-conditioned shops. The seagulls eyed the group of them beadily, saw no sandwiches, and kept on strutting.

"It's quiet here."

"Move."

Max stared at the boots and then lifted his eyes. Tom was blank-faced. Chewing gum. Both hands in jacket pockets. A jacket? Why the hell was he wearing a jacket?

Max's gut tightened. There was something in those pockets.

"Move."

He'd snitched. Told Mr Fraser that Fallowfield was in the toilets. And hadn't Jazz said it once? Snitches get stitches. That's what Jazz had said. Snitches get stitches.

He knew what was in Tom Fallowfield's pockets.

"You deaf, Farrier? The fat clogging up your ears?"

Run tall.

Max straightened his back. Scowled. Shook off the hand grasping at his elbow and turned to keep Jazz in his eyeline. Lewis was always going on about that. Never let the enemy out of your sight.

"I heard you," he said, "but I'm going somewhere. Can you let me pass, please?"

It was possibly the most he'd ever said to Jazz Coles in his life, and everything inside him felt cold and sick at daring to say it at all. He shouldn't have told. This wouldn't be happening if he hadn't told.

"No. We want a word. You're being rude again. You remember what happened last time you were rude?"

His phone beeped, and quicker than Max could move, Aidan's fingers were in his pocket, and the bright screen was swept free.

"Where's he going?" Jazz asked.

Aidan smirked. "It's his bitch girlfriend."

"He's not a girl," Max said automatically, and Jazz sneered.

"No, she wants to be a boy. You said. We're not deaf. That's pretty rude too, you know. Blowing us off for some freak bitch. Is that how bad a fuck you are, Farrier? If you did her proper, she'd not think she was a boy."

Max's chest tightened, and he reached for the phone. "Give it here."

"No," Jazz said, taking it from Aidan and twirling it lightly in one hand. "You won't need it. You can have it back when we're done talking. Now come on."

"Give it back."

"You're forgetting your manners."

Jazz's voice was getting colder. And Tom Fallowfield was getting closer. He was right up at Max's side now. Hands still in his pockets. Shoved deep. Like he was holding something.

And Max's phone started to ring.

"Should I answer it?" Jazz asked, holding it out between them. Cian's picture—that wide, toothy grin and hair burned a bright white by the sun—beamed up at them all. "Tell you what. This won't take long. Ten minutes, just the four of us. Then you can call her back."

"Him."

"Whatever."

Max saw it.

The opening.

Jazz shrugged when he said whatever. His hand loosened on the phone.

And Max struck.

Turned his hips into it. Leg up. Out. His shin smashed into Jazz's side like an axe. He dropped his guard, his right hand shooting out to catch the phone. Twisted back, elbow up. It snagged Tom in the temple. The crunch ricocheted up Max's arm. The turn dragged Tom sideways—and then the pavement was clear.

And Max ran.

The phone was still ringing in his sweaty fingers. His shoes clapped on the dry stone as he bolted. He heard shouting. His heart hammered in his chest, punching at his ribs. Run-run-run-run-run, it said.

And he did.

Ignorant of the heat. Ignorant of the effort. He simply ran. Shot through a crowded side street and then doubled back along another. Lose them. Be invisible. Shrink into the crowd, and use them. Snitches didn't get stitches in a crowd.

And only when the cinema came into view did he stop running.

Only when the cool darkness of the foyer closed around him did he stop glancing over his shoulder.

And then—

He laughed.

It sounded crazy and high even to his own ears, but the adrenaline crashing through his system suddenly made him laugh hysterically. He slumped against a column between the box office and the snack stands and nearly cackled with delirious, insane amusement.

Because he'd kicked Jazz.

He'd body-kicked him. He didn't even know what he'd done with his elbow. Lewis had never taught him to do a sideways elbow strike, or whatever that was. His thigh was complaining from lack of stretching. His elbow felt bruised.

But he'd fought back.

Okay, he'd run like crazy too, but—

He'd fought back.

And he knew from all the practice with Cian that he could do a mean body kick. He was big and heavy. Jazz would have really felt that. And Tom—Tom would have a headache for days.

Max was definitely going to die now. Definitely.

But he just couldn't stop laughing—and when Cian arrived, looking bemused, Max simply seized his face in both hands and kissed him.

"I kicked them," he said.

"Kicked who?"

"Them," Max said and started to laugh all over again.

AT HALF PAST seven, Cian said he had to go.

"Training?" Max said.

"Yep. Helping with a sparring class at eight."

Max bit his lip and followed Cian up off the bed.

"The beginners' class is at half past, right?"

Cian shot him a look. "Yeah…"

Max opened his wardrobe, fished out a tank top, and chucked it in his sports bag.

"You're going?"

"Yeah," Max said.

"Seriously?"

"Yeah."

Cian grinned. His face lit up, gleeful and bright, and Max groaned.

"Don't gloat!"

"Excuse me; I'll gloat if I want."

Max bitched about insufferable, smug boyfriends, and Cian just laughed at him before crossing to Max's corkboard and unpinning the armband.

And holding it out.

"What?"

"You have to wear it."

"I...do?"

"Yeah. Once you have one, you have to wear it."

Max swallowed. Took the slip of fabric.

And slid it up his bicep.

He had to tighten it with his teeth, and it felt a little itchy. But when it was tight, it was oddly heavy. It felt like wearing a ring for the first time.

It felt right.

And then Cian's hand was on Max's neck, soft and warm, just like the very first time. The kiss was like the first one too. Light. Gentle. A tentative expression of what Max was, in Cian's eyes.

"This isn't going to get us to boxing," Max whispered when it was over, and Cian smiled against his cheek.

"No," he agreed. "But let me enjoy it. I'm going to have to stretch to kiss you soon."

He wasn't wrong. Max grinned, rising up on his toes in a boxing stance, and had to duck in for another kiss.

"Cheat."

"It counts!"

"Cheat!" Cian repeated sternly and finally broke away. He grabbed Max's sports bag on the way and jerked open the door with a smirk. "Come on. Lewis'll kill me if I'm late."

Max followed, leaning over the banisters halfway down the stairs and yelling for Aunt Donna. The sounds of crashing on the TV dipped, and her grumpy demand that he lay off with the shouting was even louder than he'd been.

"Can you drive us to the gym?"

The sound cut out entirely. The sofa creaked, and she appeared in the living room doorway, hair on end and wearing Mum's jogging bottoms.

"To the gym?" she repeated and then glanced at Cian. "Oh, I see. Sure, I can drop you off, Cian."

"No, both of us," Max said.

Her eyes narrowed.

"Both of you?"

"Yeah."

"As in, you. You're going to class?"

"Yeah. See? Got my armband and everything."

She rolled her eyes. "Don't you go letting Lewis hear you calling it an armband."

Cian sniggered.

And then she pulled her jacket down off the hooks and smiled.

"Go on, then. Get your arses in the van."

Cian went immediately, shoving his feet into his trainers and disappearing out the front door. Max reached for his coat—and had his elbow gripped by Aunt Donna's hard fingers.

"Good lad," she said quietly.

Then she let go and was rummaging for her keys in the bowl like she'd never said a word.

Max curled his thoughts around the warm burn of pride in his stomach—at her approval, at Cian's feigned disgust at his height, at the gap between his jeans and his shoes, at the dull throb of his elbow from Tom Fallowfield's temple—and hugged it close.

Chapter Thirty-Three

August was—

Happiness.

It was a month of sheer happiness. Exams were over. Cian fractured his wrist in a bout and couldn't go to his summer training camp with the cadets. Aunt Donna postponed Max's apprenticeship until September. The gym was quiet. Half the town had gone on holiday, and the other half were working at fleecing tourists of their money. Day after day yawned out, hot and bright under brilliant summer skies. Their secret cove below the fields of dead grass became an evening joy after the picnickers had gone home and before the sun sank over the sea and vanished. In the cool, calm waters, Max finally memorised the feel of those shadow-shapes and the way Cian's freckles tasted under the salt.

It was perfect.

Max's sixteenth birthday was on the twentieth. To his embarrassment, Aunt Donna gifted him with a packet of condoms and a wicked grin. Mum shrieked and smacked her arm, and her gift was better. Max got to spend his birthday at the cove with Cian, a freezer bag full of food, and Aunt Donna's camping equipment. They spent the night in the dead fields, watching the stars through the wide open tent door. Naturally, they shared a sleeping bag. It was only manners, after Max had insisted on stargazing.

And sometime in the night, one of the condoms may or may not have been used. He couldn't possibly comment.

The first noticeable thing was that Mum had to buy him a whole new wardrobe. Not only were all his T-shirts far too large around the belly and too tight across the shoulders, but his jeans were getting shorter by the minute, and he had to constantly wear belts to keep them up.

The second noticeable thing was that Cian really, really liked well-fitting jeans on Max. Go figure.

The third thing was that Max graded a second time. Near the end of August. Lewis made him—said if he did it, Lewis would make special mention of potential and skill and dedication in that promised reference—and when Max passed that too, he earned himself another thirty seconds in the changing rooms after hours.

"You don't have to keep doing that," he said as Cian put his bra back on.

"I don't mind."

"You hate them."

"You don't. And I like the way you look at me when you see them."

The second grading was even tougher than the first—Max really was too tired for Cian after that one—and it felled him with a cold after the savage going-over Josh gave him. But the new armband felt good in a whole new way, and then Lewis insisted he get proper boxing shorts. They were a bright pattern, with Thai writing on the seat, and when Max got them home, he stripped off everything but the shorts and stared in the bedroom mirror again.

The big man was staring back.

His dad was staring back.

As early September rolled in—with a heavy thunderstorm on the first, and Cian laughingly saying they ought to go down to the harbour and kiss in the rain, like what was supposed to happen in all the movies—Max figured he must have changed, and not just in short jeans and an all-over tan.

Something in his head had changed.

"You're happy, honey," Mum said one evening when he asked. "And you know you deserve to be."

It seemed too easy. Too simple. Was a new boyfriend and a hobby all it took to be someone other than Fatso Farrier?

"But—" he started, and Mum sighed.

"Honey. Do me a favour."

"What?"

"Go and see Grandpa."

Oh.

Yes.

That might have something to do with it.

HE WENT ON his own.

It was the last day of the summer holidays, and Cian's mother had dragged him by the ear—probably literally—into town to see the dentist, leaving Max in the lurch, and with Mum's words ringing in his ears.

Grandpa and Grandma were buried in the village that they'd retired to. The village was little more than a hamlet, a stone's throw from the rocky Cornish coast, and the little chapel was the type that would have rung the bells for pirates and smugglers back in the day.

Now, Max rather doubted it had a bell.

The church was closed, the village population too small to sustain a vicar, but the graveyard was well maintained and often visited. Flowers decorated most of the graves. And by the back wall, hidden away between Mr and Mrs Fisher and Ethel Pellow, lay the Farriers.

The grave was a family one. Henry and Alice Farrier, Max's great-grandparents, had been the original owners. They'd died before Max's dad had been born. And then Mary Farrier. Grandma. And then—

The engraving was still shiny.

Max stuck his hands in his pockets and stared.

He'd been exactly once. And the hole had been open. He remembered throwing a fistful of dirt onto the coffin and crying his eyes out at home later. He'd not cried at the funeral at all. But later, at the thought of his granddad, his seafaring Grandpa with his encyclopaedic knowledge of the ocean and his devotion to the sea, being entombed in dirt...

He'd never been since.

Not once.

He'd sat in the car sometimes when Mum visited. He'd bought flowers with Uncle John or Uncle George occasionally when they'd been visiting. But he'd never stepped foot in the graveyard, not since the funeral itself.

His throat closed up tight, and Max could barely breathe.

It hurt.

It hurt all over again—a sharp pain right down the middle of his chest. He sat down on the grass with a thump. There was a little rose bush, trying to inch its way onto the grave. Mum had been last week and put down a bunch of gaudy sunflowers. Grandma's favourite.

He hadn't brought any flowers.

"M'sorry," he managed to croak, and the grave shimmered, blurry and indistinct in front of him.

He breathed.

And then again.

Then began to unpick at the pain in his chest.

"I miss you."

He'd missed Grandpa every day since he'd died. Every minute of every hour of every day. Every birthday, every Christmas, every time a ship sailed past on its way to Portsmouth.

"I've not built a single model since—"

Since.

"And I've been—"

Bad. Wrong. Fatso Farrier.

"Grieving."

Depressed.

He swallowed and pulled the threads back together in his head.

"I started boxing. Lost the weight. Mum says I look like Dad now. I think she's right."

Grandpa would have scoffed. Sentimental claptrap, he'd have said, and Mum would have fussed and told him not to be such a grumpy old man. Sentimental claptrap, Lucy! he'd insist, and then he'd harrumph at Max. I suppose you do a bit, he might have eventually agreed.

God, Max could hear him in his head as if there'd never been a funeral.

"I'm doing A-Levels. Going to—going to try. You know. Navy."

Try, Grandpa would grumble. Try, try. Trying is for failures. Farriers don't try. Farriers—

"Do," Max whispered.

The sea roared not a thousand yards from the church walls, and Max felt himself relaxing.

"I'm going to do it," he said. "Going to go to sea. Be an officer. Like you. Like Dad."

Like all Farriers ever.

And Farriers didn't let other people tell them they weren't made for the sea. Farriers didn't even let themselves say they weren't for the sea. Farriers were sailors. Born and bred. And Max was a Farrier.

Fatso Farrier.

And Fatso Farrier's grandpa had been in the war. Fatso Farrier's father had been in the Navy. Fatso Farrier had passed two Muay Thai gradings in just over a month, and Fatso Farrier was a Farrier.

And Farriers didn't try. They did.

"You'd be proud of me now," Max whispered.

The sea bellowed and agreed.

And Max hugged his knees.

"Same as you were then," he breathed.

Something deep inside his chest—and even deeper, buried away in the darkness at the back of his skull where nobody else could have found it, felt it, known it was ever there—sealed.

His lungs unlocked. His throat eased.

Max smiled into the sun and said, "Sorry I haven't been coming. But I'm better now."

Grandpa would look at him with that sharp eye and harrumph. Tell him he ought to drink more brandy. Good for the constitution.

"I've got loads to tell you," Max said. "So...so let's start with Cian."

Chapter Thirty-Four

SCHOOL STARTED THE next day.

Seven o'clock alarm. Mum had put out some of his new clothes. A proper lunch. Even a tenner for the shop round the corner if he wanted to.

"And if you need picking up after classes," she said, smoothing down his hair, "then you just call, okay, sweetie? You just call."

"I'm just calling," Aunt Donna said dryly from the front door. "Hurry up or you're walking."

Max pulled a face, making Mum giggle, and headed for the door.

He felt sick.

And he kept feeling sicker with every yard the van travelled. Every inch closer to the main gates. Every second that ticked away, and every car that wasn't blocking their route.

"You all right?" Aunt Donna asked in an unusually soft tone.

"Yeah," Max mumbled.

"You look pasty."

"Yeah, well. School."

"Your mum used your measurements to work out your new clothing sizes."

Max blinked. "Uh. What?"

"You're an inch shy of six feet, Max," Aunt Donna said as she pulled the van left and onto the road to school. It was already jammed. A gaggle of Year Sevens in far-too-large uniforms, showing their mums' ironing creases, leapt out of the way with a collective squeal. "Bet none of the other lads in your year can say that."

Max didn't answer. He was too busy watching the gates as they approached.

No sign of—them.

"And everyone," Aunt Donna said softly, "can be one inch taller if they hold their head high."

Max stared at the gates until they blurred.

He was a Farrier. And last time he'd met—when they'd meant to give the snitch some stitches—he'd kicked Jazz Coles in the ribs.

And now he was certified to be way better at kicking people than he had been then.

"Grandpa wouldn't take this shit," he said.

"Nope," Aunt Donna agreed.

"So why should I."

"That's more like. Now get out of my van. I'm late for work."

Max opened the door and stepped out.

He barely noticed the drop.

IT HAD TO happen.

And it did.

Last thing on the first day was chemistry. And Mr Fraser, true to wizened form, kept them late by twenty minutes—insistent on finishing his lesson whether the bell had rung or not.

Which meant by the time Max had stopped by his locker, picked up his sports kit, and was ready to go, the school was almost empty.

Almost.

He could sense them before he'd even pushed through the double doors into the courtyard. And there they were.

Two figures by the gate.

Jazz and Tom.

Max tightened his fingers around the strap of his bag. Took a deep breath. Squared his shoulders and straightened his spine.

Not anymore.

He was taller than both of them. Heavier than both of them. He was done getting kicked to his knees and pissed on. He was done getting slammed into lockers and being used as a football.

He was a Farrier, damn it. And nobody pushed Farriers around.

His phone buzzed and Max slid it out. Glanced down like he was uninterested.

Where are you? :(

Five minutes, meet you at the bus stop opposite Greggs? he suggested. *Just got to take care of something.*

'Something.'

Some twats.

Ahh I see. Go get them, big man.

Max smiled. Big man.

Fatso Farrier. So what. He'd never weigh in under fifteen stone again as long as he lived. And so what. He was a big man. Of course he wouldn't.

He pocketed the phone, stuck his chin in the air, and walked.

But fear wasn't so easy to shake. Every step closer, his guts felt tighter. His palms started to sweat. His fingers were shaking. His heart began to speed up, and up and up and up.

Jazz smirked.

Max's fist tightened.

"We allowed to have our chat now, Fatso?"

Max pushed out his chest.

"No."

"No? I don't—"

"I don't care," Max said, "what you want. You can piss off."

His voice was hard. It was Aunt Donna's voice. Cian's voice. Lewis's.

Max's. Somewhere from deep down in his chest, it was his voice.

And for a split second, he saw the crack in Jazz's sneer.

"If you don't leave me alone," Max said, "then I'll make you sorry for it."

"You?" Jazz scoffed. "You're gonna make me—"

"Yeah, me. Make you. Jeremy."

The sneer dropped entirely. And a cold, almost reptilian anger replaced it.

"You what."

"You're called Jeremy, and you like jazz. And you're short. I don't know why I ever took shit from you."

It was all just—pouring out. Running out of him like blood. It was Donna and Cian and Lewis, even Grandpa, everyone who'd ever told him he wasn't just a useless fat lump. It was Mr Ryhill and Mrs Pellow and Mr Fraser. Everyone who told him he could be someone.

It was Max. And it was all in there. It had all sunk in.

And now he was wringing it out.

"You're going to apologise for that."

"No, I'm not. Now back off, or—"

Tom moved.

He was quick—but Max was quicker. He lashed out, his open palm smashing Tom's arm away. Opening Tom's chest for attack.

He could have kicked him. Could punch him. Could give a warning.

But Max was running late to see Cian. And this wasn't just Tom anymore. It was every girl who'd ever ridiculed him in public. It was every boy who'd ever shoved him into lockers and walls. It was every bully at every school he'd ever been to.

It was everyone who'd ever called him Fatso Farrier.

Max's arm went up. Forearm to ear. Elbow, a jut of bone into the sky. His shoulder rolled.

And down.

Bone on bone. A crunch. A flash of red. Max fell back, feet bouncing under him. Balanced. Poised. Perfect. Tom crumpled to the pavement, his hands groping blindly at the flagstones as the blood burst out of his forehead and splattered down his face.

For the second time that summer.

And when Jazz stumbled forwards with a strangled yelp, Max—caught him.

This wasn't boxing.

This wasn't Thai boxing either.

This was his fat fingers firm around a skinny throat. A dangerous hold.

Jazz stilled, and Max tightened his grip.

Until he could feel a rabbit-fast pulse under his thumb. Until he could feel the air whistling in Jazz's throat.

"Leave it," he said and lifted.

God, he was tall. Jazz's feet left the ground. He whimpered. Wriggled.

And Max's lip curled.

Jazz Coles wasn't tough. He was some skinny idiot with a bad band T-shirt. He had snot bubbling out the end of his nose. He was called Jeremy.

Max dropped him. Kicked roughly at his thigh, and stooped down.

"If you come near me again, I'll squeeze tighter next time. Got it?"

Jazz wiped his nose on the back of his sleeve.

"Got it?" Max repeated.

His heart was pounding in his chest. And it wasn't fear anymore.

"Got it?"

The answer—the yes—was meek. Feeble. And for the first time, Max heard himself the way Jazz had always heard him. Pathetic. Weak.

That was what he had sounded like.

"Yes, what?"

Jazz's eyes came up. They were venomous—but there was something else there too. Something else Max recognised from his own reflection for so many years.

Fear.

"Yes, F—"

He raised his eyebrows.

"Max."

Max straightened up. Drew himself to his full height. Five feet eleven inches. Six foot when he stood properly.

And...walked away.

Shifted the bag higher on his shoulder and walked away. Walked down the road. Around the corner. Down the slope, and around another.

Cian was lounging in the bus stop, legs crossed at the ankles. Max stepped over them and bent down to kiss him. It was lopsided with his own smile, and Cian laughed at him.

"What's gotten into you?"

"Nothing," Max said. "Budge up."

"No room for you, big man."

"Then move, then."

Cian moved, only to sit on him.

And there, hands on Cian's arse—balance, manners, the usual—and waiting for the bus to take them up to boxing, a dull throbbing in his elbow and a sense of freedom in his blood, Max felt—

Fine.

Fatso Farrier was just fine.

Epilogue

MAX RIPPED OFF the bow tie with enormous relief.

The ceremony was over. The photographs had been taken. The confetti had been thrown—everywhere. He grinned and plucked some of the paper out of Cian's hair.

"Not quite the bouquet," Cian quipped, "but it'll do."

"Oh no," Max said. "I'm never getting married."

The last week had been hell. He'd been half convinced Mum would call the whole thing off only last night.

And now here he was, standing in the hotel gardens, watching his mum trying to teach his Uncle George how to waltz. They were both bright white—her in her wedding dress, him in his captain's uniform—and looked, thanks to the Farrier genes of pathetic dancing skills, a right sight.

"I dunno," Cian said. "You'd look good in a wedding dress."

"I look even better out of it."

"Now that is true. Dance with me?"

Max scowled.

"Please?"

"Urgh, I hate dancing."

"Boxing's dancing."

"A better type of dancing."

"Tell you what," Cian said, sidling up close. "If you dance with me—just one dance—then I'll give you another thirty seconds look in your hotel room later?"

Max bit his lip and glanced unwillingly down. Cian was binding. No way his chest would look flat in a suit shirt otherwise.

"No, thanks," he said eventually.

"No?"

"Nope."

"Why?"

"Because you get uncomfortable."

"So—"

"And I want you to be relaxed. For. Um. Other stuff."

A slow smile spread across Cian's face.

"Are you asking me to spend the night in your hotel room with you?"

"Um. Yes?"

"One dance and I will."

Max considered it. Just one dance. Okay, it would be embarrassing as hell—but a whole night in a hotel room on their own? There was no way Cian wouldn't want to do something, considering how much he wanted to do things in much more public places than hotel rooms.

"Yeah, okay. But—"

"Max? A word?"

Aunt Donna's voice granted a reprieve—although he was sure it was temporary, judging by the foul look Cian gave him when Max squirmed out of his grip. Aunt Donna had changed out of her tuxedo, albeit into a more standard suit. Max was immediately jealous.

"Why do you get to change? Mum threatened to kill me if I did."

"My wedding, fifty per cent my rules," she said tartly and jerked her head at the glass doors. "Come on. Where that loudmouth uncle of yours won't hear, eh?"

They stepped out into the gardens. Fairy lights were strung up in all the trees and the sea glittered below a full moon, calm and carefree. There was a warm breeze. It was nearly October—everything would be cold and grim soon—but the weather had held off for just that one evening.

Max leaned his arms on the railings of the little decked area and waited.

He didn't expect to hear, "It's not my place to be, Max, but I'm proud of you."

He frowned at the sea.

"Sorry?"

"The way you've turned everything around this last summer. You're growing up. And I'm proud of you for doing it."

"You...are?"

"Yes. It took a lot of guts and a lot of effort. And I'm proud."

Max turned it over in his head.

"What do you mean, it's not your place?"

"I'm hardly your mother, Max."

Max opened his mouth. No. She wasn't. But she'd been around for years. She'd bought him that birthday yachting experience. She let him hang up his ships. And she'd totally bullied him into boxing, just like Mum totally bullied him into wearing this dumb tuxedo and walking her down the aisle.

"You're good as," he said finally.

Aunt Donna said nothing.

"I mean it," he told the shimmering water. A ship was sailing across it, bound for Portsmouth, by the size of her. "You—you make Mum happy. She wasn't happy before you. That's why I didn't mind you turning up, or us moving into your house. She was happy. And—so'm I. And if you'd not pushed, I'd still be—"

He stopped.

Beside him, reed thin, Aunt Donna chuckled.

"Fatso Farrier."

"Yeah."

"Thank you."

Her voice was little more than a croak. And Max's awkward distance crumbled. He turned on her and hugged her. For the first time, she wasn't his sharp, slightly scary Aunt Donna. She was this...this blue-haired—just to annoy Mum—dungarees-wearing sparky. She was his mum's wife. His stepmum.

She was Donna. Just Donna.

She hugged him back, maybe the first time they'd ever done this, and then he let go and stepped back.

"Cian wants me to dance."

"Uh-oh. Should I clear the space?"

"Let 'em fend for themselves," he said and smiled. "And, you know. You're all right, Donna."

By the look on her face, she heard the word he didn't say.

And there was nothing more to say. Max stepped back into the conference hall, now decked out like a bad disco, without a shred of anything but determination. Get that stupid dance out of the way. And then—given it was already dark out, and Mum and Uncle George were obviously drunk—make a start on that hotel-room deal.

He found Cian dancing with one of Max's cousins and stole him back. He expected a quick sort of pretend-to-dance thing like at school dances, but instead, Cian threw his arms around Max's neck and hung on for dear life, grinning at him from only inches away.

"Oh," Max said.

"We only have to turn in a circle, and it's dancing."

"But this isn't a slow song?"

"I'm sorry," Cian said, "but do you see me giving a damn?"

"I see you being a dick."

"I see you not caring."

"It's my mum's wedding—you shouldn't be a dick at my mum's wedding."

"Of course I should. You like me best when I'm a d—"

Max applied the only known way to shut Cian up.

He kissed him.

It was a hard grip. A demand. And then it softened as Cian's fingers crept up to play in Max's hair. Someone whistled, and Max didn't care. He could feel—Cian. The hard planes of the binder. The soft sweep of his lower back. The taste of him, indescribable and uniquely his. Could feel the memory of salt, sea, and sun on his lips where they touched Max's.

He could taste summer.

Something landed on his head, and Cian broke away with a laugh.

"A sailor already!" Uncle George cheered as Max adjusted the captain's hat that had been dropped over his hair. "Need to be getting a lad in every port, though, Max!"

Max grinned, pushing the hat up.

"Well, yeah," he said. "Gonna be in the Navy, see."

"You can have me in every port," Cian bargained, coming back and stealing the hat for himself. It was far too large, and he looked so gleefully ridiculous Max had to kiss him again.

"Deal," Max whispered, right up against his mouth, and felt Cian smile.

"I do like a man in uniform," Cian murmured and rubbed his nose against Max's. "Captain Farrier. Has a nice ring to it."

Yeah.

It kind of did, didn't it?

About the Author

Matthew J. Metzger is an ace, trans author posing as a functional human being in the wilds of Yorkshire, England. Although mainly a writer of contemporary, working-class romance, he also strays into fantasy when the mood strikes. Whatever the genre, the focus is inevitably on queer characters and their relationships, be they familial, platonic, sexual, or romantic.

When not crunching numbers at his day job, or writing books by night, Matthew can be found tweeting from the gym, being used as a pillow by his cat, or trying to keep his website in some semblance of order.

Email: mattmetzger@hotmail.co.uk

Facebook: www.facebook.com/mattjmetzger

Twitter: www.twitter.com/MatthewJMetzger

Website: www.matthewjmetzger.com

Other books by this author

Walking on Water
Life Underwater (coming October 2018)
Bump (coming November 2018)

Coming soon from this Author

Life Underwater

Ashraf never thought he could fall in love. So when he falls hard and fast for marine biologist Jamie Singer, it's a shock to the system—in more ways than one.

Even if he can wrap his head around what love is and how relationships work, Ashraf's not sure this is viable. He's hydrophobic. And Jamie's entire world revolves around the sea. What's the point of trying if so much of Jamie's life is inaccessible to Ashraf?

But Ashraf has vastly underestimated the pull of loving Jamie. For the first time, he wants to face the water, rather than flee from it. He has underestimated the power of love in making people brave, stupid, or a little bit of both.

Maybe it's time to take a leap—and sink or swim.

Bump

David's pregnant.

He's always wanted to have children, and being a stepfather for the past two years has been a great adventure. There'd even been a plan to start looking into adoption and turn their family of three into four.

But now there's a bump, and David doesn't know what to do. He's spent years escaping the grip of his own body and burying the past—but there's no way he can hide from his history if he lets the bump get any bigger. It's not just his baby; it's also his breakdown.

He doesn't know if he can do this.

Also Available from NineStar Press

Connect with NineStar Press

www.ninestarpress.com

www.facebook.com/ninestarpress

www.facebook.com/groups/NineStarNiche

www.twitter.com/ninestarpress

www.tumblr.com/blog/ninestarpress